Charlie Armstrong, Surgeon

Selina Stanger

ISBN-9781521292761

DEDICATION

To the late great Phil Stanger, who kept the computer going for me against all odds

CONTENTS

ACKNOWLEDGMENTS

Many thanks to Christine Richardson of Southsea for her diligent editing, and to artist Ruth Jones of Gorseinon for her brilliant book cover design.
I could not have written this book without the help and support of my family and friends. I appreciate their encouragement and patience. In particular
Michael and Paula, Diane, Christine and Richard, for their interest and tolerance.
Wendy Metcalfe for her inspirational teaching, she told me that writing a novel was 'doable'.
Nicky, Frances, Jennie, Peter, Annette, Daphne, both Rosemarys, Julia and Jackie for their support and the 'sanity check'.

THE STORY, SO FAR

'Tom Harrison, Surgeon' was set in a small Cumberland town, enjoying a post (Napoleonic) war boom.

Tom was preoccupied with his work and reluctant to marry Nancy Graham in spite of family pressure. Schoolmistress Nancy was ready to move on, and she fell in love with a farm hand, Benjie Armstrong. He was coping with bullying and a hazardous occupation, but wanted to move away from non-skilled work on his own merits.

Tom and his mentor Dr. William Jarvis were looking for an apprentice and Benjie asked them to consider his cousin Charlie, so that he would not have to work for their grandmother, Martha, who was an agricultural gangmaster.

Nancy enticed Benjie into a hayloft and had her wicked way with him, but could not marry him as he was under age and Martha withheld permission. After a series of workplace accidents, Nancy and her father Richard felt that Benjie was unlikely to survive long enough to marry Nancy.

Led by her instincts, Nancy persuaded a bemused Benjie to elope. While the rest of the town was enjoying a bar room food fight on New Year's Eve, Nancy and Benjie ran away to Gretna using a horse and cart. Help from Tom, Charlie, Richard and his other daughters Sally and Susan made it possible. During the subsequent chase, Nancy inadvertently killed Martha's charge hand, Frank.

William and Tom reported the death as an accident, rather than manslaughter. Nancy had a few anxious moments during the inquest and Benjie's life-threatening illness, but the young couple eventually set up home in Westmorland. Benjie ran a carting business and Nancy gave birth to twins. Tom continued to enjoy a comfortable bachelor life; his parents finally accepted his skill as a doctor and came to terms with his role in the extended family. After a series of setbacks, Martha went into the poorhouse.

PEOPLE IN THE BOOK

Charlie Armstrong, journeyman surgeon
Benjie Armstrong, carter, Charlie's cousin, living in Hilltop
Nancy Armstrong, married to Benjie
Ben (Tommy) Armstrong, Benjie's son
Dickon Armstrong, Benjie's son, Ben's twin
Adam Corrie, schoolmaster, friend to Charlie
Elizabeth Corrie, married to Adam and Tom Harrison's sister

Tom Harrison, master surgeon, Charlie's mentor
John Harrison, Tom's father
Sarah Harrison, Tom's mother
Joe Harrison, brewer, Tom's older brother, living in Hilltop
Alice Harrison, married to Joe
Johnny Harrison, Joe's son
Sarah (Sadie) Harrison, Joe's daughter
Nipper, relative to Alice
George Harrison, calico printer, Tom's younger brother
Jeannie Harrison, married to George
Jack Harrison, George's son
Deborah Harrison, George's daughter
Robert Harrison, Tom's younger brother, living in Darlington
Mary Ann Harrison, Tom's sister
Henry McKay, later married to Mary Ann

Arthur Brown, innkeeper's son, friend of Tom
Edward Brown, innkeeper
Sam Brown, Arthur's son
Isabella Brown, Arthur's wife

Richard Graham, blacksmith
Kit Dawson, blacksmith, friend to Charlie
Sally Dawson, married to Kit (Richard's daughter)
Chris, Ricky, and Frances Dawson, Sally and Kit's children
Susan Graham, schoolmistress, twin to Sally

1 THE SENIORS

It felt very different, wrong. It was the same ale house where Tom had spent many happy evenings and it was almost a second home. Everything was very familiar; the smoke-stained ceiling, the sawdust on the floor and the dim corners where anything might lurk. The new billiard table stood proudly in the centre of the room, with a noisy crowd of young men around it.

Tom's own tankard shone brightly above the bar, next to his brother George's. The tankard was always a welcome sight, and Arthur's greeting was a welcome sound.

"The usual, Dr. Tom?" asked Arthur, reaching for his tankard.

"Yes please," answered Tom, clearing a space on the least sticky part of the table. The ale house had gone downhill a bit in the eight years since he qualified as a doctor, but he had his loyalties and his customers knew where to find him. The call that he was dreading could come at any time.

"How are your friends at Hilltop?" asked Arthur. "The mail coach driver said that Benjie seems to be having problems with his carting business these days. I also heard that..."

"You shouldn't listen to idle gossip. Benjie and Nancy are fine, why wouldn't they be?" put in Tom, quickly. He had a feeling that things at Hilltop were not quite right but didn't want to encourage discussion, especially by Arthur.

"Here's to the new senior surgeon!" said Arthur, changing the subject and raising his tankard. "How is Dr. Jarvis finding retirement, all that way down south?"

"He said in his letter that Blackpool was much the same as here in Gorton, only the rain is slightly warmer. He is getting used to living at his sister's but I didn't even know he had a sister," said Tom.

"We'll all miss him," said Arthur. "Though you and Charlie will look after us very well, I am sure," he added hastily.

Tom wasn't quite so sure. He tried not to think about his misgivings as he moved his chair to make room for his brother George. They had to move their table further into the corner to make space for the billiard players. Charlie and Adam were taking on all comers. Adam was a lefthander, so he took up a lot of space and looked particularly awkward as he took a shot from the corner.

"Corrie by name, Corrie by nature. I have never seen anyone quite so corrie-fisted," said George. His children had told him that the young schoolmaster could use a cane with either hand.

"Is dad coming tonight?" asked Tom.

"He said that he might come along later," answered George.

"Mr. Harrison's place has been empty a few times recently," said Arthur, "I hope he's keeping well."

"Just prefers his own fireside sometimes," explained George, "I can't imagine getting like that."

"Dr. Jarvis used to like staying in, towards the end; just lit his pipe and settled for the evening," said Tom. "How is Isabella?"

"As well as can be expected," said Arthur with a shrug. His wife had been 'enjoying' ill health for several years.

"I have some new tonic," said Tom, opening his bag hopefully. "Perhaps that would help."

"Nothing seems to make any difference," said Arthur who saw himself as long suffering. Isabella saw things differently.

"If you are sure," sighed Tom as he closed his bag again.

"No word from the blacksmith?" was Arthur's parting shot as he went back to organize the bar staff.

That was why the place felt wrong tonight, thought Tom. The next room, where the old men usually sat, was strangely silent.

"Where are all the older men?" asked Tom, not thinking that he had spoken his thoughts out loud.

"You are the older men now," replied Charlie to Tom and George. "It's time you moved into the snug where you belong, give us a bit more room to play billiards. Your friend the carpenter has been sitting there on his own for ages."

Tom and George took the hint, and moved into the next room. The dark panelled room was very cosy and they could see quite well by the firelight. The snug was much more comfortable than the bar room, with oak panelling, plenty of space, and staff bringing the drinks. The nights were drawing in; it seemed a very pleasant place to be but it seemed very quiet, only the carpenter sat staring morosely into his beer.

"You took your time. I thought I was going to be on my own all evening," grumbled the carpenter.

"We didn't expect you would be on your own," said George. "Where is everybody?"

"Edward Brown is away on one of his mysterious jaunts. The rest are staying at home or poorly; some of them have gone to a better place," said the carpenter, lifting his eyes heavenwards.

"Like Blackpool," quipped Tom, trying to lighten the mood.

"How's the blacksmith?" asked the carpenter, who was determined to be gloomy. Richard Graham had suffered a stroke during the previous winter.

"Richard seems a lot better now, he hardly needs his stick," answered Tom.

"He could have another stroke any time, couldn't he?" asked the carpenter. "He is nearly sixty now, he's had a good innings."

Tom didn't want to think about it; he had expected the older generation to always be there, especially Richard Graham. Arthur came to join them, bringing a welcome jug of ale.

"I'd have expected to see the blacksmith by now. Come to think of it, I haven't seen the young blacksmith either," said Arthur.

"Isn't Kit with Charlie and the others?" asked Tom. There had seemed to be a lot of young men, but he could not remember seeing Kit.

"No sign of either of them," said Arthur, "I hope nothing is wrong." His words fell heavily into the silence.

"I see you have fetched young Dr. Charlie back from his travels," said George. "I didn't think he was ready to qualify yet."

"He isn't." explained Tom. "He has another six months before his twenty-first birthday so he wasn't best pleased at being fetched back. Charlie was enjoying his journeyman travels and had hoped to go to London. "But with Dr. Jarvis gone, I needed him here."

"I'm sure there is a lot more disease than there was in the old days," said Arthur. "Folks have no stamina these days, the least little thing sees them off."

"The mill workers never seem to be very healthy," added George.

"I heard that there was measles in Carlisle," said Arthur, "and that always puts a lot of people underground."

"We've always had typhoid, consumption, cholera and the rest and I could have managed with another journeyman and a lad to run errands. I wouldn't have needed to bring Charlie back, but the government has brought in a lot of extra paperwork for us to do," explained Tom.

"I hadn't thought," said George. "We had to go to that new fancy office and answer loads of questions when our new baby was born and we didn't have to do any of that with the others. I can't see why the government can't mind their own business instead of finding extra work for people to do."

"You see the problem," said Tom, "The registrar needs us to check the dates of birth for him; it all takes time and the new death certificates are a nuisance."

"The vicar won't bury anybody without a death certificate," grumbled the carpenter, "and it plays havoc with our schedules."

"That's right. And then we sometimes have to register the death as well, if the family is too upset. That is why I needed Charlie's help; another journeyman would be useless, as he wouldn't know the local people. I tried, but there was a bit of a backlog with the vicar being difficult and folks getting upset and wanting the funerals quickly," said Tom.

"What is the use of it all? They even have to fill in a form to get married. The bride and groom have to say how old they are, and what they do for a living and even what their fathers do for a living. The fathers like to show off a bit, so if a farm worker helps with the slaughtering he calls himself a butcher. That upstart shoemaker calls himself a cordwainer, as if he only worked fine Spanish leather, instead of being a bootmaker like his father before him. It takes all the joy out of the ceremony and wastes good drinking time," added the carpenter, whose daughter was married recently.

"I heard that folks who were in a hurry could get married at the office instead of the church, and they wouldn't have to wait for the banns," said George, "but nobody has, yet, not even Dissenters."

"I thought that things would be better with the new young queen on the throne. Queen Victoria behaves with decorum - she is not like those dreadful uncles of hers. Or her mother! I thought her government would have some good ideas, not have us fiddling about like this. I even heard that they wanted to have a list of where everybody lived. I just can't see what for. It's just the nanny state taken too far!" said Arthur.

"I suppose they want to keep track of us all so that we can pay more taxes," sighed George.

"Don't worry, I am sure it will never happen," said Tom. "It would be much too difficult to do. Lots of people live in more than one place. I sometimes live at my father's house and sometimes at the surgery."

"I think that you spend most of your time here," said Arthur, "This is your real home."

Tom thought that the ale house was his favourite home, nice and warm, with good company and plenty of ale. No awkward customers, paper work, or clerks asking difficult questions. They settled into a companionable silence, but he could hear snatches of conversation from the billiard room next door as the young men waited to take their turn.

"Are you still a journeyman, Charlie?"

"Yes, I can't qualify until I am twenty-one, next year."

"You've qualified, haven't you, Adam?"

"Yes, I'm headmaster of my own school, with a schoolhouse to live in and a wife to look after me. My mother said they didn't have room for all my books at home."

"And Kit's a master blacksmith now, engaged to Sally Graham. He has his feet under that table all right."

"Yes, Kit's done very well."

"You were apprenticed before either of the others, weren't you? Are you a bit slow or something?"

"I'm not a 'bit slow'. Just a few months younger, that's all."

"I suppose you aren't walking out with Susan Graham yet, then?"

"Give it a rest will you or I will come over there and…"

Tom sighed as he settled down by the fire. It must be very hard for Charlie, but it was only a few short months before he qualified and was in a position to ask Susan to marry him and nothing could possibly go wrong in that time. Tom tried to ignore further snatches of conversation.

"Is that Doctor Tom in the snug, with the other old men?"

"Yes, they're just putting the world to rights."

"Big man, compared with his brother. Same height but twice the girth!"

"They used to be the same size, but Dr. Tom got bigger over the years."

"Is there something wrong with him, to get to that size?"

"No, he did it all himself with a knife and fork."

Tom was wide-awake by now and on his feet, on his way to the billiard table, but hadn't decided whose ears to box. The door opened suddenly and Kit rushed in, shouting for all to hear.

"We need a doctor at the forge right away, Mr. Graham has had another bad turn!"

2 THE BLACKSMITH

Charlie and Tom went out of the warm ale house into the cold wet street, struggling to keep up with Kit who was striding ahead. Charlie felt that Tom should have gone on his own, as he was the senior doctor, but Tom said that Susan would need Charlie to be there. Kit said that the blacksmith would want to see both of them and would they please hurry up.

The streets were very dark, but they knew the way so well that they did not need the help of the new gaslights in the main streets. The houses looked warm and cheerful with the firelight and occasional candle. Tom and Charlie struggled against the wind and rain; it looked as if it would be a hard winter. The wind took Charlie's breath away, as he tried to keep up with Kit, and for once in his life he had nothing to say.

He remembered how kind the blacksmith had been to Kit and himself when they were two young boys, just out of the poorhouse. Richard Graham had never looked down on them, and always treated them as if they were part of his family. The big blacksmith was an important man in the town of Gorton, and Charlie could not imagine life without him.

***

The house was very subdued when they got there, no noisy welcome from Richard and his family. The kitchen fire was out, and the house plunged into gloom. Kit had managed to carry the old man up the narrow stairs to his bed - Charlie and Tom would have struggled to carry him between them. The stairs were narrow and Tom nearly missed his footing when he arrived at the landing earlier than he expected. There were two bedrooms on this floor for Sally and for Richard, and a very narrow staircase leading to the attic bedrooms for Kit and for Susan. Richard was propped up in his large sturdy bed; in the candlelight Charlie could make out a linen press and a bedside table. Richard sat very still, his left arm at an unnatural angle and the left side of his mouth twisted. He opened his eyes when he heard them come in, his mouth moved but they could not make out a word he said.

Sally was kneeling on the rag rug on the floor, with her head on the side of the bed, weeping as if her heart would break. Kit took her in his arms to comfort her and she clung to him. Charlie would have liked to hold Susan in his arms, but remembered that he had a job to do. Susan was ignoring everybody and rushing about tidying the room, which did not really need any tidying. Tom stood back and let Charlie take the lead.

Charlie took Richard's pulse, and checked for fever. He asked what had happened, and Kit answered in his slow voice that Richard had collapsed when he got out of his chair downstairs, but had been caught before he hit the floor. Charlie looked at Tom, who indicated that he should continue.

"You have had another stroke, more severe than the last one. Your speech might come back, and the use of your left arm, but we can never be sure what will happen. I'm so sorry," said Charlie, hesitantly.

Richard made writing movements with his good hand, and Susan rushed off and brought a slate and piece of chalk. Richard struggled to write, but the words 'How long' were clear enough by the light of the candle. Tom and Charlie looked at each other and Tom shook his head.

"It could be as little as a week," said Charlie, trying to keep the sob out of his voice. "It could be longer, as you are such a big strong man. I have known cases where…"

The blacksmith was writing on his slate again – 'Fetch Lawyer'.

"We'll send for him in the morning, I think you should get some rest now," soothed Susan.

"We'll call again tomorrow," said Tom, "I'll leave a sleeping draught in case you need it."

The blacksmith wrote in large letters on the slate, 'NO MORE LEECHES'.

"If you're sure," replied Tom, "I think they did the trick last time."

As Charlie and Tom took their leave, they noticed the final words on the slate 'Fetch Nancy'. Richard obviously thought he would die soon, and wanted to see his eldest daughter before it was too late. Nancy was married to Charlie's cousin Benjie; they were living in Hilltop and Charlie had not heard from Benjie for a while.

***

Sometime afterwards Tom and Charlie were by the fire in their kitchen at the back of their surgery. Originally a house like all the others in the terrace, the front room had been turned into an apothecary shop. The large shop window held intriguing bottles of coloured liquid and lotions and potions to cure all ills. There were always remedies to ease joint pain, indigestion and colic but the rest depended on the season. Currently the cough mixtures were replacing summer medicines like calamine lotion, and it looked very much a work in progress.

The shop had a small dispensary behind screens that also served as a consulting room. It was out of sight of the queue of people in the shop but not out of earshot, although in a small town everyone knew what was going on anyway. Tom said that he always got extra customers if there was to be a tooth pulled or a boil lanced. Charlie also took bets in the dispensary, as he would often unofficially run a book on the outcome of some local event. The kitchen room was large, with a door leading to the narrow stairs to the bedrooms. There was an archway leading to a scullery that jutted into the small enclosed garden, and a door leading to a room that started off as a study but got rapidly full of the things that no respectable doctor could do without. Their charwoman would not go near the study as she said that the skeleton gave her the creeps, and she fought a losing battle trying to clean the rest of the house.

The kitchen table was used for dining, writing, and for mixing medicines when the doctors wanted to keep the mystery about the ingredients. Sometimes a specimen from a jar in the murky study was brought in for dissection. And sometimes all these activities were in progress on the table at the same time.

Charlie loved the place, ever since the doctors had collected him from the poorhouse to be their apprentice. His future of agricultural labour or stone breaking had previously looked bleak. When they were not so busy he would see if he could do something about the study to give them more space; he might even take a look at the attics and cellar; they had not been visited for years.

Charlie was beginning to feel better, partly because Tom had given him a nip of brandy for medicinal purposes.

"We've really caught up with all those certificates now you are back," said Tom. "I used to spend ages trying to work out which kind of natural causes to put on the form."

"It's difficult in the cities as well, when nobody knows anybody, and sometimes people just drop dead in the street. If we were really stumped, and the patient looked as if they were over thirty, we used to say death was due to a worn-out constitution," said Charlie.

"Fair enough," said Tom, as he was nearing thirty himself and feeling a little tired, "and if they were younger?"

"Visitation from God. Nobody argued with that one, they just went home to pray and left us alone," said Charlie.

"And how's your old friend the registrar?" asked Tom.

He remembered the registrar as master of the poorhouse when Charlie had been a small boy who was always in trouble.

"He is managing a bit better now; he has hired a second clerk," answered Charlie. "The registrar has to attend all the inquests; this takes up a lot of his time. One of his clerks used to work for the Coroner; he wasn't very good at writing notes so he got sent to the registry office. The other clerk has just left school; he is a bit out of his depth but should pick things up in a week or two."

"I'm sorry I had to bring you back early, but I needed you here, the other journeymen were very lazy compared to you. Your work is really good, but unfortunately you are not allowed to practice until you are twenty-one. The months will just fly past, and then you will be officially recognized as a partner," said Tom.

It seemed a long way off to Charlie, but he did not feel quite so undervalued as he had done earlier in the evening, he just thought that he could have skived a little more. Charlie's mind went back to their visit to the forge.

"Do you always tell patients when they are going die?" asked Charlie. "Doesn't it make the end of their life more difficult?"

"In most cases it is a kindness," replied Tom, "so the patient can put his affairs in order, make his peace with God and man. Some patients can't handle the knowledge, and we spare them."

"How do you know the difference?" asked Charlie.

"I get it wrong sometimes," answered Tom. "You can learn the skills for your trade in a few years, but learning about people takes a lifetime."

***

The following day was a Sunday, with the shop closed, and no planned visits. There was no word from the forge, so Tom and Charlie made their way there in the afternoon. The fire was burning brightly, casting a warm glow over everyone. The kettle was boiling and Sally was busy making toast.

Charlie had always tried to put a finger on the difference between this kitchen and their own. Both houses served as places of work, but the blacksmith's house seemed to be more of a home. There was a parlour kept for 'best' and hardly ever used, but the kitchen was the real heart of the house. The stone floor was always swept whether it needed it or not; there were no cobwebs and everything was in its place. No books or papers graced the table; perhaps it was the 'woman's touch' that made the difference.

Richard was never happier than with his daughters, holding court around the tea table, offering hospitality to all comers. Sally was engaged to be married to Kit, but had not set a day yet. Nice girl, Sally, but a bit dull and she liked to stay at home. The lovely Susan was different altogether, and Charlie looked forward to a future with her. But how could they think about the future at a time like this?

Richard was in his chair; he seemed very much in command of himself although his left arm was hanging uselessly by his side. He gave a lopsided smile when he saw Charlie and Tom.

They had all spent time in the cosy kitchen in the past, regaled with tea and toast, only now it seemed very different. The room looked just the same, the fire with its hob, fire irons, coalscuttle and toasting fork. The dresser stood proudly against the wall, all the plates on display and the brass was shining. The table, chairs and stools were in place but Sally and Susan were not bickering, and were strangely silent. Richard looked haggard and his speech was slow and slurred.

"You're looking better than you did last night," said Tom.

"I'm feeling better," said Richard, "but I appreciate the warning you gave me last night. I thought I had all the time in the world to put my affairs in order."

There was a gasp from Sally; her face was away from him but Charlie could see her shoulders shaking. Susan sat white faced and silent, her fingers working away frantically at her knitting. Charlie felt his own eyes welling up.

"I need to settle my debts, show Kit a few things about the way the forge is run," Kit nodded slowly, "and show Sally how to balance the books on Lady Day at the end of the year." Sally stopped, the toast on the end of the fork. "I have arrangements to make, that I have been putting off for a while," said Richard. "I would like to see Nancy again before…"

He stopped before he completed the sentence; Sally's latest piece of toast was covered in flames. This gave them all a little diversion; Sally, Susan, Kit and Tom were all very busy with the offending slice of toast. Only Charlie heard Richard say that he would have liked to see one of his daughters wed.

"I think that might be possible," said Charlie, slowly.

"The vicar likes the banns for four weeks and can't be doing with licences," said Richard. "I don't think I'm fit enough for the ride to Gretna."

"I think the rules about weddings have changed, the registrar was telling me," said Charlie.

"It would have to be within the week," said Richard. Sally's toast waved very close to the fire again, but another disaster was averted.

"With some kinds of licence, a couple could get married in less than a week," said Charlie. "I will find out tomorrow morning."

Susan managed to pour the tea without spilling much, but Sally's toasting fork was very wobbly. Susan filled the silences in the conversation; she was frantically scraping toast before it was fit to be buttered.

3 THE BRIDESMAID

The following morning, Susan bustled in the kitchen, thinking of the thousand things she had to do. First, clear up after breakfast in case anybody called. Then rush over to the school and ask if she could have leave of absence for a few days. Adam Corrie had sent a message saying that she could stay home as long as she needed, and not to worry. But Susan still needed to set her class some work to do, and she couldn't quite remember her plans for the top group.

"Slow down," said Richard, "you have washed that plate three times."

"So I have," said Susan, with a giggle, "I was miles away, thinking of what I needed to do this morning."

"Sit down and have a cup of tea with me," said Richard, "the rest of the world can wait."

Susan poured the tea, and then opened the door for the first visitor of the morning. Elizabeth Corrie asked how Richard felt, and told him that he was looking well even though he wasn't.

"I am so sorry, I meant to come over and sort things out for my class. I hadn't realized that it was so late," said Susan, who felt that nobody else could teach her class quite as well as she could.

"Don't worry about the children, Adam and I will manage," said Elizabeth.

"I meant to set them some work to get on with, to make it easier for you to keep an eye on them," said Susan.

"There will be a few absent this week, so the classes will be smaller," said Elizabeth. "Adam says that some of the children are staying home to help with the potato harvest, so he thinks there's room for your younger children in my classroom and the rest in his."

"Some of my older ones are not very good with joined up writing yet," said Susan. One or two were not very good with any kind of writing.

"I think I know the ones you mean," said Elizabeth. "God did not mean everybody to be a scholar. They can come to me if they're struggling; we have plenty of space. I can always borrow some of the older girls if I need help, they can read stories to the children for a bit."

"Thank you so much," said Susan, "I don't mean to impose." She thought how kind and helpful Adam and Elizabeth had always been. Life had been very different for her elder sister Nancy when she had been teaching at the same school. Nancy had to shoulder too much responsibility, as the other two teachers had been elderly and lazy. There had been larger classes in those days but some families had moved away from the town now, looking for work.

"Just don't give it another thought, we'll manage," said Elizabeth. "Not as well as if you were there," she added hastily, "but we'll get by. You are a friend as well as a colleague, and I am sure you would do the same for me."

Elizabeth left, declining the offer of a cup of tea, saying that she would come and visit another time. Susan felt much better as she drank her second cup of tea, and tried to stop her worries crowding in on her.

***

The morning passed quickly, with a surprising number of well-wishers dropping in to see them. It was a welcome distraction for Richard as he was an active man who was not used to sitting about. He seemed to be more tired than usual after lunch, and Susan recommended that he should take a nap. This would give her time to worry about where everyone would sleep.

Susan had made her own bed up for Nancy, and wondered if it would be big enough if Nancy's husband Benjie came with her. Benjie had never been a big man, but Nancy was the size expected of a blacksmith's daughter, as was Sally. Susan moved some of her possessions into Sally's room and wondered whether the bed would be big enough for both of them; it seemed to be much smaller than the last time she and Sally had shared it.

As Susan came downstairs with an armful of linen, she heard the murmur of voices. As she went through to the washhouse she saw her father in serious conversation with the lawyer, papers all over the table. Susan went back upstairs, closing the staircase door behind her. She was very tempted to sit on the stairs and listen, but decided she was too old for such things now.

Susan turned her attention to finding somewhere for Nancy's sons to sleep; they would probably come with Nancy, as they were too young to be left on their own. The truckle bed would be big enough for two seven year olds sleeping head to tail, but she could not remember where it was. By the time she had found the bed, dusted it off and moved it to her own room she was tired, hot and cross. After another search for linen and blankets, Susan went back downstairs for a cup of tea.

The lawyer had gone and Richard was fast asleep with a smile on his face.

More visitors arrived in the evening, after work had been finished for the day. Richard had an enjoyable time instructing George and Adam how the quoits team should be run in the future. Richard obviously intended that they should have the benefit of his experience when selecting a team – he knew which men talked a better game than they played.

Charlie arrived a long time after the others left; he was intent on checking his patient's progress, but Richard wanted news from the registrar first.

"Did you see him? What did he say?" asked Richard.

"A couple can get married by licence, they only have to wait seven days," said Charlie. "I know it isn't quite what you were looking for, but it is quicker than calling the banns."

"No sooner than seven days?" asked Richard.

"There is an Archbishop of Canterbury's special licence, but it might take a few days to arrange. They have never done it before and Canterbury is a long way away," said Charlie. "You will just have to stay with us for another week."

"You doctors will have to see to it that I do," said Richard.

"Susan, my love," said Charlie, turning towards her and going down dramatically on one knee, "will you marry me?"

"Of course I will," said Susan, "now get up off that stone floor, you'll catch your death of cold."

"You make me very proud," said Richard with a beaming smile.

"Are you ready to name the day?" asked Charlie. "It might be more sensible to marry after I have qualified, just in case something goes wrong."

"What could go wrong?" asked Richard.

"I might do something unforgivable, and Dr. Tom might turn me out," said Charlie.

"Dr. Tom might fall off his fine horse, and his family could sell the practice," said Susan. This was unlikely as Tom's horse, Thunderbolt, never quite lived up to his name and his progress was usually fairly sedate.

"There might be a cure for consumption and no more epidemics," said Charlie, "People would live forever and the work would dry up."

"I can't see that happening," said Richard.

"They could change the rules about doctors qualifying," said Charlie, "The new Queen seems to make up new rules all the time, according to Edward."

"That is a good point," said Susan, "as a married woman, I'd not be able to keep my job and bring in money. If I am engaged there is no problem."

"It might be difficult to manage on a journeyman's wage," said Charlie," and if Susan were widowed, she would have no capital from my share of the practice."

"Her dowry would help you," said Richard. "Nancy got the horse and cart, Sally will inherit the forge, Susan will have two cottages."

"I had no idea!" said Susan as it had not occurred to her that she would have such a generous dowry.

"A cottage in North Street, and the one that backs on to it; the lawyer's conveyancing them for me. You could rent them out, live in one or knock through and make one grand house. I think they might need a bit of work though," said Richard.

"I am not sure that I would like Susan to be bringing in more than I am," said Charlie. "A man has his pride."

"Can we sleep on it?" asked Susan. "See how practical it is? Just in case there is more work than we think."

"See what you think in the morning, Sally and Kit will be back by then," said Richard.

"Where are they?" asked Charlie, who had forgotten.

"They have gone to bring Nancy back from Hilltop," answered Richard. "I thought you would have gone with them, to see Benjie." It was a long time since Charlie had seen his only cousin.

"I'll see him soon enough when they arrive," said Charlie, "I had visits to make and I'd promised to see the registrar."

If Charlie had known what was about to happen to Benjie, he would have dropped everything and gone to Hilltop with Kit and Sally.

***

Kit and Sally arrived much later than expected and Susan and Richard were sitting dozing by the dying embers of the fire. Nancy had arrived without her family and in the half-light she seemed very tired. Richard decided that it was too late to make any plans that night, and ordered everyone off to bed. Susan was secretly glad, but took the opportunity to talk to Sally when they were alone. Sally's room looked very cluttered; it took a while to get ready for bed because there was no direct path from the door to the bed. In addition to a tallboy the room seemed to have all the coffers and spare chairs from the rest of the house. Susan thought that there had been more space between the furniture when they shared the room in the past.

"Nancy came on her own, then," said Susan, "and I spent ages finding that truckle bed for Dickon and Tommy."

"Nancy didn't want them to miss school, so they stayed at Hilltop. They were hoping to stay with Joe Harrison and his family – you remember

Tom's brother Joe? Dickon and Tommy have grown a lot since we saw them last, but Dickon's still very much the larger twin. Tommy prefers to be known as 'Ben' now, says that as the eldest he should be known by his grandfather's name," said Sally.

"Nonsense! He should have the name he was given – he can't pick and choose." Life would be easier without two seven year olds running about, getting each other into mischief. Susan saw enough children at school.

"You seem to have brought a lot of your things down from your room, there is hardly any space left."

"I had to make room for Nancy and her family. Couldn't Benjie come? Everyone would have liked to see him."

"He was all set to come, but the squire wanted some work done at the last minute. He particularly wanted Benjie, rather than Nipper. He says that it's an honour, working for the squire so much, but Nancy says it's a real nuisance. Benjie seems to be at their beck and call all the time, but he can't turn the work down. The squire could make it difficult for a carter to make a living at Hilltop, could turn others against Benjie. It's an old-fashioned place, several villages joined to make a town, and the squire is still very important, not like here."

"How does Nancy put up with it?"

"She just grits her teeth and gets on with it, but she doesn't like the squire's new wife. 'Milady', they all call her. She was nobody, just a lady's maid, and then she married the squire before his first wife was cold. Can't we put all those books somewhere else?"

"They are to go back to school. I will call in when I've time. Can't you move over a bit; you are taking up more than your share of the bed."

"I'm squashed right up to the wall as it is. Did Charlie go to the registrar? What did he say? How early can Kit and I get married?"

"Seven days apparently, by licence rather than banns."

"That's wonderful! I would love to get married next week. That hayloft will be very draughty in the winter."

"Hayloft? What do you want that for?" asked Susan, "Oh, I see!"

"We couldn't bring ourselves to be intimate under father's roof, it wouldn't be right. Don't tell me you haven't! You are a prim and proper spinster, aren't you? Not like your sisters," said Sally. They both giggled, remembering that Nancy and Benjie had enjoyed the hayloft before they married.

"We thought about it. But I worried about what would happen if… We couldn't support a family on a journeyman's wage, and I couldn't hold my head up in the town."

"So you don't want to bring your wedding forward? We can't have our double wedding then?"

"We've not quite decided yet. It might be more sensible to wait, perhaps save a little money and set the date for April. It's only a few months, and nothing is going to change in that time; we will be an engaged couple, and the hayloft will be available."

"You will have to get all your stuff out of this room before my wedding. I can't start my married life with the room in this state."

"I suppose not. Please can you move over a bit more. You might need a bigger bed, Kit is much larger than I am." Sally did not think that was the case, but was much too tired to argue.

4 THE BEST MAN

Charlie was walking on air, all the way home. The walk back to the forge in the morning was a different matter as he had a glass or three with Tom to celebrate the engagement, and felt a bit befuddled. Charlie arrived at the forge to find Richard explaining the finer points of running the forge to Kit and Sally; he was talking loudly and tracing intricate patterns with his good arm as they discussed the new wrought iron work. Kit was looking puzzled, but Sally was nodding slowly and there was no sign of Benjie or Nancy.

Susan was waiting impatiently, dressed to go out; obviously she had been waiting for Charlie. He could not remember making arrangements to go anywhere with her that morning, but supposed that he must have done.

"Sorry I'm late," said Charlie - he had no idea what time he should have been there, "but I had one or two things to attend to. How's the patient?"

"I'm as well as can be expected," said Richard, waving them off. "I slept fine so off you go with Susan and I will see you later."

"You've forgotten where we were going, haven't you?" asked Susan.

"Er..." said Charlie, looking up and down the street and trying to remember.

"I will save you the trouble of guessing. We're looking at the cottages, to see what sort of a state they are in. We don't have the key yet, but can have a look at the outside, and through the windows," said Susan, and they set off at a smart pace.

"Did Benjie arrive last night? I haven't seen him for ages."

"Nancy came on her own, Benjie had to do some work for the squire," said Susan, turning up a narrow side street, "Now one of the cottages is on this street and the other one around the corner. They may be fit to live in, or they may need some work."

She stopped outside a small two storey terraced house. The door opened right onto the street and there was a dirty window next to it. Paint was peeling off both the door and the windows, and the window upstairs was broken. Charlie went forward to look through the window and nearly overbalanced when he found a metal grill under his feet. Through the grill he could see another broken window, leading to a gloomy cellar. There was debris piled up against this basement window and some of it had blown inside.

Susan thought that the other cottage might be better, and they went around the corner to have a look. The second cottage backed on to the first; they shared a wall and neither of them had a back door. The wind blew leaves and dust along the street, rattling against the doors.

"The main room is here," said Susan, indicating the window, "and the door opens straight into it. I think there's a small scullery the other side of the door but it has no window so I can't see properly. There's a bedroom and a tiny box room upstairs."

"If there's no yard, there can't be any outhouses. What about the…" asked Charlie.

"The privies are shared with the neighbours," replied Susan, indicating a couple of small buildings at the end of the row. These, and the other cottages, seemed in reasonable condition.

Susan peered in at the window; Charlie assumed that she was looking at room sizes and furniture. He tried to look as if he was taking an interest but it was all women's stuff. Charlie's head ached, his stomach churned and he leaned against the door to steady himself.

The door suddenly gave way and clouds of dust and a pigeon flew out. In silence they propped the door back in its place, neither of them wanting to go inside.

"We could live at the surgery, in Dr. Jarvis's old room. I could give it a bit of a tidy."

Susan had seen the downstairs of the surgery, so she could only imagine what the upstairs would be like and suppressed a shudder.

"We could start off in Kit's attic, as he will move into Sally's room after the wedding. Nancy is in my room at the moment, but she will go home soon and we'll get it back." At least Kit's attic is clean, she thought.

"Perhaps if we waited a few months, like we were going to. Then we could save up and we'd have more choice. Time to have some work done on these cottages, or even spring clean Dr. Jarvis's old room. Or we could rent somewhere else, even better."

"It would be more sensible to set a day in April," said Susan, "my father will be ever so pleased, even if we are not getting married straight away." She hoped so, anyway.

"Benjie used to say that engaged couples have extra privileges."

"Sally was telling me. I had no idea!"

"So you won't be getting married until the spring," said Kit when they got back to the forge. "I had hoped that we'd have a double wedding next week."

"Sorry," said Charlie, "we've set the day, though."

"That is really good news," said Richard. "Sally is to be married straight away and Susan to be married in the spring, so all my daughters will be settled. Kit is supposed to be off to the registry office to see about the licence, but it seems he is dragging his feet."

"Charlie, I don't suppose you could come to the registry office with me and show me what I need to do? I don't even know where it is," asked Kit, hopefully.

"Just down the road, I'll show you," said Charlie. They set off towards the main street, waving at Arthur who was standing on his doorstep watching everyone go past. "I suppose everyone will know where we are going now."

"Why did you decide to wait to marry?"

"We wanted to wait till I qualified as a doctor and earned a man's wage. And Susan said we should save up first, I like to spend my money and enjoy it; it seems as if I have a lot to learn. Do you save any money each week?"

"I don't know; I suppose I do. I just hand my wages to Sally, and she gives me some back for beer and tobacco. It makes life easier, I would only lose it otherwise." He had a long lecture from Richard about charging more for wrought iron work if it was fancy and took a long time. Kit did not see why there was a problem, but Sally would sort his prices out for him and keep track of customers who were late paying. It seemed that there was a lot more to being a blacksmith than just working in the forge.

"I could save a bit out of my wages, and keep quiet about the money I make from betting," said Charlie. He thought Susan might be a bit funny about the betting, so he never mentioned it to her.

The registry office was a couple of rooms in the town hall; the corridor outside served a waiting area. The larger room had bookcases and shelves, and a splendid large desk for the registrar. From his elevated position he could see through the open door into the smaller room where his two clerks were working, writing silently in big books.

"How nice to see you both." said the registrar, "What brings you here? I hope nothing has happened to poor Mr. Graham." He remembered Kit and Charlie as small inmates when he was in charge of the poorhouse. He would never admit it but they were favourites of his; they gave him endless amusement getting in and out of trouble. He had been pleased when they were offered apprenticeships, and had wished them well when they left.

Kit stood tongue-tied, feeling as if he were twelve years old in the master's office again. Charlie explained that that they had come to arrange for a wedding between Kit and Sally Graham as soon as possible.

The registrar looked over his glasses at Kit, deliberately sharpened his quill and made a great show of selecting a new form from among the piles of paper on the desk. Then he smiled, and asked them whether they should see the vicar about the banns first. Charlie explained that four weeks would be too long to wait, and Kit wanted to get married by licence as soon as possible.

"I can arrange that for you; it will be the first wedding at this office. I will have to study the rules and find out about the ceremony. I expected lots of Dissenters beating a path to the door, but there have been none so far. Are you really in so much of a hurry?" asked the registrar. Sally had always been a big girl, but you could never tell.

Kit stood there and blushed, and Charlie stepped in to say that Mr. Graham had requested it in view of his own declining health. After they completed the formalities, the registrar had a final word with Charlie.

"You never would let him speak for himself, or even get a word in edgeways, even when you were lads," he said. "Now off you go. If I remember rightly it is your turn for infirmary duty this morning and you are nearly an hour late already."

***

Richard seemed to rally during the week before the wedding; his speech was still slow, he never regained the use of his arm but he enjoyed seeing all the visitors who came to wish him well. People were bringing wedding presents almost as soon as Kit got back from the registry office; it was surprising how quickly the news had got around. Arthur offered the use of his ale house for the wedding party, saying that since the big quoits match was over for the season, Richard could dance as much as he wanted.

Charlie arrived on the night before the wedding, to take Kit to the ale house for his last night of freedom. Richard said that he would stay at home and save himself for the wedding party the next day, and that Charlie had to bring Kit home early and in a reasonable condition.

In the event, it was Charlie who needed bringing home as the townspeople provided a never-ending series of drinks, and Charlie made the mistake of trying to keep pace with Tom and Kit. Adam had more sense, and Charlie thought that he was getting to be a dull old schoolmaster already.

Outside, Charlie felt decidedly wobbly and a bit queasy so he had to go and lean over the wall. That's better, he thought, as he wiped his mouth with the back of his hand, it must have been a bad pint. Probably the seventh or eighth, rather than the first. He had noticed the same thing before at other ale houses. He wondered if any doctors had done any research on the problem, and whether they were in a fit state to write up the results.

He could hear people taunting; they seemed miles away and nothing to do with him.

"Look at Charlie Sawbones!"

"Can't hold his drink!"

"Still has a lot to learn from Dr. Tom."

"Maybe that is why he isn't a proper doctor yet."

That has nothing to do with it, thought Charlie, it was a bad pint, that was all. Only medical people understand.

But Charlie found that he was having trouble walking up the street as his feet had a mind of their own, so Tom and Kit half-carried, half-dragged him home.

5 THE WEDDING

Susan was pleased that her father had rallied, and ignored Charlie's warning that he might be hanging on for the wedding. She had come back to find that Nancy had taken over the kitchen and was making dinner, without asking her advice on anything. Nancy seemed changed somehow, when asked, she said that everything was fine at home, but there was no spring in her step. Susan decided to ask Sally about Nancy's grumpiness later, when they were on their own.

After dinner, Nancy said that Susan should wash up since she hadn't done much that day. Susan was a bit miffed at the way she was ordered about, but she gritted her teeth and got on with it as she had been brought up to be polite to guests. When the carpenter and lawyer arrived she described the cottages and allowed herself to be sent out again with the carpenter to see how much he needed to do. The lawyer came as well, as he hoped to haggle the price down because the cottages required extra work. Susan had hoped that Nancy would go home soon, now that their father's health had improved, but Nancy had other ideas. She decided to stay for the wedding and oversee the arrangements – she didn't want it to be a shambles like George Harrison's wedding. Susan thought she had a point; certainly Elizabeth Harrison's wedding to Adam Corrie enjoyed the same happy chaos.

Susan thought that an extra pair of hands would be useful, if only Nancy didn't insist on making all the major decisions. Susan found things more and more difficult, so she went back to work earlier than expected, telling the Corries that her father's health was much improved, and she could be fetched if needed. She returned home after work to find that Nancy treated her like a ten-year-old, sent her to wash her hands because tea was nearly ready and even asked her if she had a nice day at school!

To try and keep her temper, Susan took every opportunity to go out of the house on various errands, spending long hours with the carpenter at the cottages and even longer hours with Tom's sister-in-law Jeannie Harrison, the dressmaker.

***

The wedding day dawned, Richard's good humour was infectious and the family was all smiles even though Benjie had not been able to come to the wedding. They were very surprised and pleased to see Tom's sister Mary Ann; she had been a close friend of Susan and Sally when they were younger. She had been able to take a day's holiday from her work as a milliner in Carlisle. Mary Ann was tall, slim and dressed in the very height of fashion. She did not need the suffocating stays that her upper-class clients wore, so she was able to smile.

Nancy said that it was a pity that Mary Ann would get more attention than the bride, but Susan told her sharply that Mary Ann was only trying to sell a few hats, and everybody had to make a living. Mary Ann had brought fashionable hats for Sally and Susan, little bits of nonsense with feathers and flowers, but Nancy was heard to mutter that a plain serviceable bonnet was good enough for anybody.

Sally took her father's arm as they set off to the office, Susan walking behind her as bridesmaid. Mary Ann persuaded Nancy to walk with her in third place, carrying Richard's stick in case he should need it later. They found a lot of people at the town hall, and wondered what was going on, but it was the wedding that had drawn the crowd. The registrar was on the steps, with a big smile on his face, beckoning them in.

The people in the corridor and office made way for them to pass through. Susan was amazed to see so many people; she thought it would have been a very quiet affair. Kit was looking very self-conscious in his new city hat, but Charlie was parading up and down and enjoying himself. He turned, removed the hat and gave a little bow when he saw them, and drew a round of applause. Nancy said that that there was nothing wrong with a good sturdy cap and fancy hats only encouraged people to show off.

The registrar took charge of the short ceremony, saying the same beautiful words as the vicar used at a church service but without the sermon and all those hymns. Susan thought of Charlie, fidgeting in a long church service because he wanted to go fishing afterwards.

The registrar flourished the certificate for signing, and everybody moved forward to have a look at this strange new piece of paper that usually kept its mystery hidden away in the church vestry. Kit hesitated, looking at this official certificate in the registrar's unmistakable copper plate handwriting, wondered if he should sign himself as 'Christopher' and whether he could still remember how to spell it, and whether the space on the paper was big enough. And would the wedding still be legal if he got it wrong? He sat there wondering if he could use the old form of his name (Xofer), until the registrar kindly told him to write 'Kit' on the line he was pointing at.

"Thank you, Kit and Sally," said the registrar, as Charlie was about to scribble his name on the form. "Now it is your turn, Charlie. Don't rush your signature, your handwriting was never very good and a doctor's training hasn't helped. Best writing, please, take all the time you need." He looked at Charlie sternly over his spectacles.

Charlie made a great pantomime of hunching over the desk like a naughty schoolboy, sticking his tongue out of the corner of his mouth and laboriously writing his name. Susan was laughing so much that her hand shook as she wrote her own name a few minutes later.

***

The wedding party, their friends, and half the town continued the celebrations in the ale house which had been tidied up and bedecked with ribbons and flowers. The food was plentiful, the ale flowed, and everyone looked forward to dancing on the green behind the back door. Susan started looking for the fiddler to provide the music; she remembered seeing him earlier in the evening. Nancy recollected previous occasions when the ale had flowed too freely near the fiddler, so she searched the outhouses and found him asleep, instead of on duty. She was none too gentle when she woke him, and sobered him up by dipping his head in the horse trough. The guests thought that it was part of the entertainment, and roared their approval.

Susan felt very proud of Nancy and forgot about their many disagreements during the week. All the same, she looked forward to Nancy's departure on the stagecoach in the morning and life returning to normal.

The fiddler still looked a bit dazed, but knew his tunes so well that he could play them without involving his brain. Everyone enjoyed the dances; they progressed up their sets, giggling at the mistakes. The registrar was dancing with his wife who was as short and round as he was; everyone admired his fancy footwork.

Richard sat at the side, enjoying the music and tapping his feet. He was keen to join the dancing, but was persuaded to sit still and watch until Nancy went off to chivvy the servant girls. She came back to find her father with the dancers, leaning on his stick and shuffling his feet while everybody danced around him.

An interval was called, to give the dancers a rest. Nancy saw that the fiddler was heading off to the ale again and asked him to play something quiet for everyone to listen to while they got their breath back. He took one look at Nancy and struck up a very dignified minuet, keeping his face very solemn. A ripple of laughter went around the room, but there was more to come.

The registrar bowed to Richard, and asked him to dance; he declined but Charlie was already on his feet. The registrar took the female part with many elaborate twirls, fluttering of eyelashes and flirting with a borrowed fan. Charlie played his part manfully with many stately bows to his partner and the audience and flourishes of his hat.

***

The evening drew to a close all too quickly, and the wedding party was ready to set off home, so Tom had volunteered to stay and deal with any casualties from the evening revels. There always seemed to be fighting after weddings, people remembering previous events and having scores to settle. Harvest festival and New Year were even worse, needing both doctors to patch people up, and volunteers to take them home in the wheelbarrow afterwards. Men did not fight after funerals; the women sometimes fought over possessions but rarely came to blows.

Richard did not seem too steady on his feet, but refused to go home in the wheelbarrow – said that he had never needed the wheelbarrow and did not intend to start at his time of life. Nobody argued as he was a big man and it would have taken at least two men to take him up the road, more if he wasn't willing.

Sally and Kit led the way, and Richard followed with Charlie on his left and Susan on his right. He was able to walk quite easily with support, and soon they were all singing the melodies from the evening's music. Susan walked steadily but Richard and Charlie were capering as they went up the road. Nancy came last, carrying Richard's stick and trying not to laugh.

Richard was still singing as Kit and Charlie helped him up the stairs, thanking them all for giving him the best day of his life.

***

The house was ominously quiet the next morning when Susan got up early to light the fire; she missed hearing her father set up the forge for the day's work. She went upstairs, knocked on his bedroom door and waited. When there was no reply she went in to find Richard lying in bed, and she knew that he would not wake up again.

6 THE WAKE

When Charlie saw Susan on his doorstep he knew what had happened, and they walked back to her home in silence. They found Nancy and Sally clinging to each other, and a white-faced Kit working in the forge.

Charlie's examination told him that Richard had died of a massive stroke, which could have happened any time. He thought it was a shame that Richard had been so adamant about the leeches but he reassured the others that nothing would have made any difference. Charlie told them that Richard might have died earlier in the week had it not been for the wedding. The house seemed eerily quiet without the blacksmith's booming voice, and Charlie realized that the sisters were wondering what to do next.

"These days we have a lot of extra paperwork to do, whenever anyone passes away. I will fill in one of these new forms for the government, and then I will go and see the registrar and come back to you. Do you have any idea how old your father was?" asked Charlie. They all shook their heads.

"Do they really need to know?" asked Susan anxiously.

"I don't see the point either," said Charlie. "I'll just make a guess like I usually do."

Charlie wondered about this all the way to the registrar. What was the information for? Was it just to fill books to line office walls somewhere? Could people look in these books and find out everyone's secrets? It seemed very much of an intrusion into people's lives just to make extra work for clerks somewhere.

The registrar was sorry to hear the news and as he carried out his duties he seemed very different from the man who danced at Sally's wedding.

"It must be very sad for you to register the death of a friend," said Charlie.

"In a town this size it is usually a friend, family, or someone I know," said the registrar. "The saddest ones are the baby deaths, as it seems such a short time since I registered their births."

"I suppose so. We always know which babies are not going to thrive, although we look hopeful for the parents," said Charlie, "and an epidemic or hard winter carries off the very young, the old and the weak - it is a hard time for everybody."

"Here, take this piece of paper to the vicar, then the funeral can be arranged," said the registrar kindly. "Richard had a good life. He didn't get to his three score and ten," (Charlie wondered whether he had) "but he lived to see his daughters settled."

"Even though it was expected, it's still a shock," said Charlie.

"He'll be missed," said the registrar. "Nobody will look after those girls quite like their father did."

"Kit and I will do our best," said Charlie, "and Benjie of course."

"Ah yes, has your cousin Benjie arrived yet? I expect Nancy will be all right, but I always thought that trouble sought Benjie out," said the registrar.

"I expect he will be here for the funeral," said Charlie. He thought to himself that when trouble came looking for his cousin, Benjie was always ready to meet it halfway.

Charlie got back to the forge to find Susan in control of the situation.

"Sally and Nancy are laying father out, so we do not need the midwife to come in and do it. Arthur came in with his condolences," (he must have seen me go in to the town hall, thought Charlie) "and I asked him to let everyone know, since he'll do that anyway. Can you ask the vicar to call, and the carpenter?"

As a bemused Charlie was dispatched on errands, he thought that Richard's daughters could look after themselves very well.

***

A constant stream of people came to pay their respects; the kettle was hardly ever off the hob during the three days before the funeral. Everyone had good things to say about Richard, which made the girls' eyes well up again and again. The last visitor was the lawyer, who brought some papers and a little box and proceeded to read the Will.

"The house and the forge are to go to my daughter, Sally Dawson, and her husband, Kit. I leave the business as a going concern and I am sure that they will make a success of it," read the lawyer.

Sally and Kit did not look so sure.

"It is such a big responsibility," said Sally. "What happens if we have problems?"

"I don't know what to do!" Kit looked shattered. "I haven't enough experience." Suddenly he was the town blacksmith, and he still felt as if he was an orphan just out of the poorhouse.

"You have been doing the job for the last six months, you'll be fine," said the lawyer. "There are no debts but you may need to replace the horse and cart sooner rather than later. I can advise on money matters and Hamish can advise on your craft, but I don't think you will need to call on him."

They all remembered Richard's friend Hamish, the blacksmith at Gretna, and Kit brightened up considerably.

"To my eldest daughter, Nancy Armstrong, I leave my wife's jewellery," read the lawyer and handed her the box.

"I had not expected anything, I received my inheritance when I married," said Nancy. Her father had given her a horse and cart, which enabled the young couple to start a carting business. She looked as if she wanted to open the box, but was restrained enough to leave it for later.

"To my daughter, Susan Graham, I leave two cottages: 15 North Street and 15 Back North Street. Repairs are in progress and have been paid for," read the lawyer. "Susan, your father recognized that you are engaged to be married to Charlie Armstrong here, and has given his consent to the marriage. You are still under age; your father said that I could be your guardian, acting for you in money matters in the meantime. Or you could choose someone else."

"It is my responsibility as your elder sister…" started Nancy.

"I am more than happy for my father's lawyer to be my guardian," said Susan, quickly.

"I was only trying to help," said Nancy. "If you don't want me…"

"We appreciate your help, but I think it makes sense to have a local lawyer acting for Susan, for, er… tenancy agreements and that sort of thing," said Charlie diplomatically, trying to break the tension.

Susan's glare at Nancy took in Charlie for good measure. Sally tried to keep her face straight but found it difficult.

"Although now you are a woman of means your guardian may advise against marriage to a young upstart like me!" said Charlie, and good humour was restored for a while.

***

Later that evening the immediate family and close friends followed local custom and took part in a vigil on the night before the funeral. The open coffin was on the kitchen table as there had been no way to carry it up and down the narrow stairs. A solemn Kit was adding more coal to the dying fire, as it was going to be a long night with Nancy returning to a previous argument.

"I understand that normally women don't go to funerals, but I think that it should be permissible for older married women to attend," said Nancy.

"Why don't they go to funerals?" asked Sally." I've always wondered."

"They just don't, that's all," said Kit. "Perhaps they are too busy getting ready to look after the guests afterwards."

"They might weep and wail and the funeral would lose its dignity," said Tom.

"I don't weep and wail," said Nancy. "Younger girls might, but older women know how to behave." She continued to sew furiously.

"Just one hint of a tear on a fair cheek would set everybody off," said Charlie before Susan could speak her mind. "We would all be weeping and wailing and then where would we be?"

The thought of some of the town dignitaries weeping and wailing amused Sally.

"Mr. Graham would have decided who should go and who should stay home," said Tom, "but we can't ask him for advice any more. There are fewer and fewer older men to guide us."

"We'll have to muddle through," said Sally, "and we still have the lawyer and the carpenter."

"And the registrar," said Charlie, "and old Mr. Brown at the inn when he isn't away on his travels. Then it's down to you, Tom, and George and Arthur to guide us young ones." He pantomimed being a schoolboy to reinforce the point.

"We're all sober citizens now, although some are more sober than others," said Tom. "I find it very disconcerting to have no older generation to blame when things go wrong."

***

As the night wore on, the group became weary; Sally was leaning on Kit's shoulder and had fallen asleep, and he had been snoring for some time. Tom was sitting by the fire contentedly smoking his pipe; Charlie was not used to sitting still for any length of time and was beginning to fidget.

Nancy was sewing furiously, getting more and more annoyed with her work; Susan watched her with increasing irritation.

"What on earth are you doing, Nancy?" asked Susan, "Wouldn't you make a better job of it tomorrow in daylight?"

"I am sewing my mother's jewellery into the hem of my cloak, if you must know," said Nancy, who did not want to admit that the task was not going as well as she had expected. "If I'm to go home by stage coach I must try and keep it safe from highwaymen. Though I can't see why…"

"We've been through this," said Susan, "We can't spare Kit to take you home, he has too much work to do as it is. And the journey to Hilltop is getting too much for poor old Dobbin. You agreed yesterday to go on the stagecoach."

"Perhaps I could stay a bit longer until Kit is free to take me," said

Nancy.

"You won't want to be away from Benjie and your two little boys any longer than necessary," said Susan, "I am surprised that…"

"I am sure Benjie will arrive tomorrow for the funeral, and take you home in your own horse and cart," said Charlie who was finding it hard work keeping the peace. He hoped he heard a faint knock on the door, but wasn't sure.

"I don't see why you don't all get some rest if you've nothing to do. I will sit up with father since I have all this sewing to do," said Nancy, with the air of a martyr.

"I've plenty to do," said Susan, "I have things to get ready for tomorrow, and I need to start the bread as I won't have time later. I have my responsibilities."

"I'll make the bread and get things ready," said Nancy, "You just go to bed."

"You'd better finish your sewing," said Susan, "you'll need lots of time if you are to do it properly. If it is anything like your usual efforts, it will fall apart and mother's jewellery will be scattered all the way up the road." She stormed off to the scullery.

The knocking on the door became louder, and Charlie was ready. He tossed a coin, covered it up, and asked Tom to call.

"Heads," said Tom, without thinking.

"You win," said Charlie, "if someone needs a doctor, I'll have to go." He opened the door to admit the carpenter's son.

"We need a doctor quickly; my youngest brother is ever so poorly." said the lad. "He has a fever and the light hurts his eyes."

Charlie picked up the doctor's bag, kissed Susan goodbye and hurried out of the door asking whether the boy had any new spots.

7 THE SEDUCTION

Charlie was out of the door before Tom got a chance to question him. He wondered whether the coin had really come down 'heads'. And who had won, and who had lost.

"Shouldn't you be going with him, as senior doctor?" asked Nancy.

"Charlie is a good doctor, ready to qualify when he is of age. He can do the work just as well as I can," said Tom. "It looks as if measles has arrived in the town, five years since the last time. This is not good news, and both Charlie and I will be really busy quite soon."

"Do you let Charlie do visits on his own then?"

"Of course I do. And he has responsibilities at the infirmary; Charlie is doing all Dr. Jarvis's work now. When you left town to get married, Charlie was a new apprentice, little more than a child. He is now a man, doing a man's work."

"I suppose so, I hadn't thought. Sometimes it seems like yesterday and sometimes it seems a hundred years ago. But don't you want to make sure he is doing things properly and not making mistakes?".

"He will make mistakes, we all do. But I must let him do things his own way and learn from his mistakes. He has not got as much experience as I have, but he is much better at explaining things to the patients."

"Is that important?"

"Very important, because the patients need to believe in their treatment if they are going to get better. Some of the old ladies thought that Dr. Jarvis made them better just by looking at them."

"Was that possible?"

"In a way. If the patient has faith in the doctor and is optimistic, it makes his body stronger to fight the disease. Now I have told you one of our secrets, I hope you'll keep it to yourself. The patient's confidence is stronger than anything in the doctor's bag," said Tom with a smile.

"So if I said anything, people would stop believing in you and all just keel over," said Nancy. "For goodness sake don't tell Arthur, it would be all around the town in no time."

"I wouldn't tell Arthur, or my sister Mary Ann, I have a living to make. I wouldn't even tell Susan or Sally. I know they are grown women now, but I expect they still gossip," said Tom, keeping his voice low.

"I suppose my sisters are grown up now; they still seem very young," said Nancy, lowering her voice and moving nearer to Tom. Susan was clattering about in the scullery and would not have heard them anyway. Sally and Kit slept through everything.

"People like to do things their own way. You remember when Adam Corrie was a boy? Everyone tried to make him use his right hand instead of his left; they thought it would make life easier for him. He did his best, but got quite confused at one time. But your father knew what was wrong, and made a really good quoits player of him. And Adam plays billiards with his left hand; he's the only one who can get the better of Charlie. Uses a pen or the cane with either hand apparently," said Tom, "Perhaps Susan needs to do things her own way. She has done very well up until now." Susan had started to thump the bread dough about; she seemed to be taking out all her frustrations.

"I was only trying to help; I didn't think it would upset her. She got so cross when I offered to advise her about the cottages, as good as told me to mind my own business."

"Imagine if one of your relatives came to stay with you and ordered you about in your own kitchen! How would it make you feel?"

"I must have really upset her, I must go and apologise," said Nancy as she went to the scullery to make her peace.

Tom smiled as he heard the thumps stop for a while, and then resume more quietly as the pummelling became gentler. He was glad that all was well again, but thought that the bread might not be as good as it would have been with the sisters still at war.

"Now come and tell me about those lads of yours." said Tom. "They must be quite big by now. Your father would be proud of them."

***

The following morning Kit had harnessed the horse, the sisters draped the cart in black and Dobbin stood quietly as he seemed to know that he was taking his master on his final journey. Nancy was fretting because Benjie had not arrived, but felt reassured when Tom said that he would represent her at the funeral. When the remaining pallbearers arrived the coffin was lifted on to the cart and the procession set off with Kit leading Dobbin. Tom and Charlie led the procession of mourners walking towards the church.

Tom, Charlie and Kit sat in the front row, so they did not see the church filling up, with men standing at the back and in the porch. This was the church where Richard and all his family had been christened, going back many generations. The church had been enlarged over the years, whenever anyone had the funds to do it, but for all its changes it stood on the same spot. Never a warm church with its stone walls, it seemed particularly cold that day, as if it was taking some of the warmth and life out of the town. After the ceremony, Tom saw many people he did not know, but thought that some must be blacksmiths by the way they carried themselves. Quoits players from all over the county had come to pay their respects; even Hamish and his sons had made the journey from Gretna.

Some of the crowd melted away from the graveside but a good proportion made their way back to the forge with Tom, Charlie and Kit. The womenfolk had already arrived including Tom's mother, sister and sister in law. Nancy and Susan had managed to cooperate long enough to prepare refreshments for the guests; surprisingly there was enough bread, rum butter, tea and beer to go round. The tea table in the kitchen looked the same as it always did, except for the empty chair that everyone avoided.

Hamish asked Kit to show him the forge, and Kit looked a bit more cheerful when they came back sometime later. People were still standing around the edges of the room, trying not to look at the empty chair so there was a sharp intake of breath when Hamish sat in it, followed by a sigh of relief. Of course Hamish hardly ever visited, and would not know that the chair was the especially large one that Richard always used.

"This is a blacksmith's chair; it needs to be sturdy because we are usually very big. Try it for size, young Kit, you're the blacksmith now." Hamish stood up and waited for Kit to gingerly try it and look around apprehensively in case Richard came back and asked what he was doing in the blacksmith's chair.

"Mr. Graham is not going to need it anymore," continued Hamish. "I suggest you use it instead of one of these other flimsy chairs, unless you want to give your carpenter a lot of work."

"That's alright by me," said the carpenter hopefully.

"I must be on my way now, Mr. Dawson," Kit realized that Hamish meant him, "but remember what I have said."

The guests started drifting away at this point, to their houses, their work or the ale house. Tom and Charlie had several calls to make, but promised to return later in the evening.

***

Tom returned later to find Kit sitting in the blacksmith's chair, comforting Sally who was sitting on his lap, and he thought that it was a good job that the chair was sturdy. Charlie and Susan sat close together in the inglenook, but Charlie was preoccupied with the next crisis to threaten the town.

"The carpenter's youngest son went to Carlisle with him a few weeks ago, and now he has measles. It will spread quickly through the town like it did last time," said Charlie. "You can help by spotting it when the children are in school and sending the offending child straight home. You can send the brothers and sisters home for good measure as they will have measles next."

"How do I know if it is measles?" asked Susan, "Some of the children might pretend to be ill to get the day off."

"It doesn't matter too much if they are sent home on suspicion," said Charlie. "Measles can kill children or damage them. These are the signs to look for…"

Tom smiled to himself as he went to look for Nancy, he found her in the scullery, washing up, tears streaming down her face. He placed a comforting hand on her shoulder and she looked up.

"Sally has Kit to comfort her, and Susan has Charlie, but there is nobody here for me." said Nancy, uncharacteristically sorry for herself.

"I'm here, "said Tom, taking her in his arms and getting soaking wet in the process.

"I'm fond of you Tom, we grew up together and you have always been good to me. But I was hoping that Benjie would be here for the funeral at least. Arthur will have sent word to the world and its grandmother, so Benjie obviously can't get away from work."

"You'll have to make do with second best, but it is a pity that Benjie couldn't get away, we would all have liked to see him."

"The squire keeps him so busy, and he can't turn him down or nobody would give Benjie any work. It is so difficult, the squire is very powerful because we are so far out in the country and I just don't know what to do."

"It is not like you to be at a loss. Is there something else worrying you? You can tell me – doctors know how to keep secrets," he continued when Nancy hesitated.

"It's the squire's new wife – Milady we all call her. She is the one who keeps asking for Benjie, it has to be him, he can't send Nipper, and it's not just carting work."

"What does she ask him to do?"

"All sorts of things. Sometimes it's moving furniture in her bedroom, and then the next week she wants it all back the way it was. Once she even asked him to lace up her corsets, said her maids could not do it tightly enough. Asked him to admire her waist and compare it to mine. There is no comparison, she's a lady and I'm built like a blacksmith's daughter," said Nancy, looking down at herself.

"I think I'm built like a blacksmith's daughter too," said Tom, running his hands down his waistcoat, making Nancy laugh. "Surely you don't think she can steal Benjie's affections."

"I'm more worried about the squire finding out and misunderstanding. There has been talk already. What can I do?"

"Perhaps you should send somebody with him when he goes; Nipper, one of the lads, or even yourself."

"A chaperone, to make sure that she does not entice him into her hayloft and have her wicked way with him?"

"Us men are poor weak creatures," said Tom, "and easily enticed into haylofts."

"Is that right?" asked Nancy, taking Tom's hand and leading the way.

Tom was no virgin; there had been the occasional barmaid or farm girl and some of his lady customers preferred to pay in kind rather than coin. He had always wondered what it would be like to make love to Nancy, but they seemed to be just two old friends comforting each other and nothing more. Afterwards they cried in each other's arms for the loss of their childhood, their youth and their innocence.

"I heard a noise in the hayloft," came a voice from underneath the ladder.

That's Charlie's voice, thought Tom as he tried to suppress his laughter.

"Just the cat, I think."

Tom and Nancy were both laughing by now; it did not help when Tom mouthed the word 'miaow'.

"I'm sure I heard a giggle, it looks as if the hayloft is occupied. Is there somewhere else we can go?"

"Kit's old attic is available and more comfortable."

Tom and Nancy held in their laughter until the footsteps had gone.

"I feel better than I've done for a long time. I wish I could stay here instead of going home on the stagecoach tomorrow," said Nancy.

"You should go home. It looks as if Benjie needs you more than ever," said Tom, knowing that relations between Nancy and Susan would soon get strained again.

In the years that followed he wished he could have taken his words back and kept Nancy safe with him. Benjie was beyond help.

8 THE FLIGHT

Ben thought that he could see the whole of Westmorland from his vantage point up the tree – some of the familiar fells had snow on them already even though it was only October. When he looked down, he could see everything in his own world quite clearly, the houses, the stream, the roads, the inn, the church and the farms. He wished he could climb higher so that he could see the whole of England, but he was not quite as big as his friend Johnny Harrison. At least they had got away from Johnny's annoying little sister, Sadie, who always followed them about.

Ben and his twin brother Dickon had spent a lot of time with Johnny's family while their mother was away visiting her hometown. He had heard that that his aunt had got married and his grandfather had died, but couldn't remember what either of them looked like. He wished he could just stay up the tree forever, but knew he would get hungry sometime.

"There you are!" said Sadie. "Mam says you have to come down for your tea and Tommy has to go home."

"Don't call me Tommy," said Ben, "My name is Ben."

"Your Mam calls you Tommy!" said Sadie, "You have to come down now!"

"Why does she call you Tommy?" asked Johnny.

"After my godfather," said Ben, "but I am the eldest son and should be called after my grandfather. Tommy is my middle name."

"I shall tell Mam that you won't come and you'll both get into trouble," said Sadie, running off. "Dickon went home ages ago."

Ben and Johnny slowly climbed down from the tree, their peace shattered.

***

Ben was not prepared for what he found when he got home. His mother was kneeling on the yard floor, crying over what looked like a bundle of messy red rags. He slipped as he came closer, and found that he was following a trail of blood. Spot was still harnessed to the cart but he was standing in the wrong place, and Ben could not understand why neither his father nor Nipper were there to look after him. Worse still, Dickon was standing, white faced on the back doorstep neither moving nor speaking.

Ben was about to shout to his brother to ask him what was happening, but he heard heavy footsteps behind him and some sixth sense told him that he should be quiet for once in his life. He started towards the back doorstep, and something told him to take the longer route behind the cart rather than going straight across the yard. He heard the constable and the squire's men talking to each other but did not dare turn around.

"There she is, arrest her now!"

"What's the charge?"

"Murder."

"But if he lives?"

"Unlawful wounding. But he'll die and then worse than just murder, it could be petty treason given the circumstances."

Ben was behind the cart now, edging along the wall, towards his brother.

"We can start taking the goods now, everything is forfeit and there's nothing to stop us."

One of the squire's men took a step towards the cart, and Ben held his breath.

"Not without a warrant from the magistrate. Mr. Percy and Mr. Peregrine are with him now so it won't be long."

"What have I done? What have I done?" There was a wail from Ben's mother.

"Just take Mrs. Armstrong, the local jail will do for the time being."

"And Mr. Armstrong?"

"No hurry, he can be collected later."

Ben realized with a shock that the bundle in the yard was his father. Or had been his father. He stifled his gasp and moved closer to his brother, hoping that he could not be seen in the half-light. Ben wanted to come out and fight the squire's men but felt that the family was in enough trouble.

"Shall I take this lad to the workhouse now?"

"Wait for the warrant, it won't be long. We need to find the other one; he must be hiding here somewhere."

"I need some help over here!"

"I can't believe that you can't arrest one weak woman by yourself!"

Nancy was causing quite a disturbance and was obviously not going to go quietly. Hopefully she would keep the three men busy so that the boys could escape. Ben held his breath as he quietly reached the doorstep, took his brother's unresisting hand and led him out of the front door. Ben was keen to find out what had happened but realized that it was not a good time to stop and ask questions. Uncle Joe would know what to do, and would make everything all right again, if only they could reach him before the squire's men found them.

***

Hidden away in a quiet corner of the inn where Uncle Joe worked, Ben realized that nothing would ever be all right ever again. This wasn't the big room with the large cheerful log fire where they usually went. It was a small bare room that looked as if it had been a storeroom at one time; it was hidden away at the end of a corridor and had one small window, high up on the wall. There were cobwebs everywhere and the room looked as if it hadn't been swept for years. There were a few sacks in the corner where they were sitting, and they didn't smell very nice.

Ben wanted to go back home, to get something to eat and make sure that everything was as it should be. He needed to see for himself that his mother and father were all right, but Uncle Joe stood between him and the door and didn't seem to be in a mood to answer questions.

Ben tried not to think about what his mother might have done, or what had happened to his father. Instead he wondered whether Joe Harrison was a real uncle, because he did not think they had any relatives living close by. His school friends seemed to have lots of relatives to look out for them, and Ben had always felt that it wasn't fair. Perhaps he was distantly related to Auntie Alice, as half the town seemed to be. All the women seemed much more friendly with Auntie Alice than they were with his mam; they were popping in to talk to her all the time. Some of the men were friendly to his dad but the squire's men did not seem to like him much for some reason and the squire was a very powerful man. Even the schoolchildren whispered a bit and Sadie said that his family was not liked, mainly because they were 'not from round here' but she hinted at other reasons.

Auntie Alice came in with small beer and a plate of bread and dripping, which distracted Ben from their whispered conversation.

"What's to do?"

"Nipper will fetch his cart when it's dark enough…"

"No sign of the other one then…"

"Must have been taken already…"

"They didn't waste much time. I suppose they're looking for…"

"We must get them away as soon as possible…"

"Tonight?"

"It has to be; they can't stay here. Is the man still living?"

"I don't know; they've called…"

"It looks bad then. And Nancy?"

"Shh! Little pitchers have big ears."

Ben turned away from the conversation and tried to make it look as if he was giving his undivided attention to the bread and dripping. He noticed that his brother Dickon had hardly touched his slice while Ben was starting his third.

"Eat up, lad, you'll need to keep your strength up for the journey," said Uncle Joe, but there was no answer from Dickon.

"Why, where are we going?" asked Ben. He knew they were going somewhere but he could not imagine a faraway land where there was no bread and dripping.

"Somewhere safe," said Joe.

Ben gulped. Did that mean that he wasn't safe at home anymore? What had his mother done to his father? He remembered that once she threw a whole pile of plates at him, one by one, and then sat down and cried because they had all missed him. And then they had cuddled and made friends afterwards, so whatever she had done she never really meant it. But now they couldn't make friends afterwards because his mother was in jail and his father was …

"But what about dad? He might not be dead! Perhaps he will get better – he will need us to help him," said Ben. Dickon had still not spoken.

"There is nothing we can do, lad," said Joe, shaking his head.

Ben shivered. His mother never meant to hurt anyone, it wasn't fair if she went to jail for something she didn't mean to do. Another thought, even worse, came to him.

"They hang murderers, don't they," said Ben, chewing his lip and trying not to cry.

"They never hang anyone in Westmorland, we haven't enough people to spare in this god forsaken place," said Joe. "Now, I need you both to be brave. The cart is ready for our journey, but I want to make it look as if we are just carrying sacks of goods. It is very important that nobody knows where you are going."

"Where are we going?" asked Ben, "Do I have to go in this sack? It smells horrible."

"It'll keep you warm, lad," said Joe, "Now, not a sound until I tell you it is safe."

Ben wanted to argue again, but thought better of it as Dickon was already in his sack, allowing Joe to carry him without protest.

***

Ben would remember the journey for the rest of his life. The first part was worst, as he was hidden in his evil smelling sack, under a pile of other sacks that were even worse. He could feel straw under the sack, and wondered if it had been changed since the pig went to market. Ben felt every bump and pothole on the road because he did not know when they were coming and could not brace himself. All he could hear was the horse's hooves and the annoying squeaky wheel on the cart so he held on tightly and hoped that he would be allowed out soon as he still had some questions he wanted to ask.

It was dark when Ben and Dickon were allowed out of their sacks; Ben could see that Dickon was just lying very still and silent. He nudged him with his foot and felt very relieved when his brother shuffled out of the way. Ben sat up; pushing the sacks to one side, but the night was so cold that he chose the warm smelly sacks over the chilly night air. He couldn't even see where he was, in the pitch darkness.

"Where are we?" asked Ben.

"Not even half way yet," said Nipper, "if you go to sleep it will make the journey go quicker."

"Why do we have to go?" asked Ben.

In reply, Nipper gave him an apple with the warning not to drop anything off the cart onto the road. Ben ate his apple slowly, core and all, he was surprisingly hungry even after he had eaten more than his share of bread and dripping earlier. He tried to ply Nipper with questions, but Nipper was silently concentrating on the horse and cart and not saying much. There seemed to be an unlimited supply of apples; Ben thought that each one tasted a little sharper than the previous. Ben's belly started hurting as he ate the last apple so he lay back in the sack trying to ignore the fact that he was feeling sick.

When Ben woke up it was just before sunrise and he was surprised that he had managed to sleep. Dickon was lying in the cart. Ben could hear his slow steady breathing as if he was asleep, but Dickon's eyes were wide open. The weather had changed, there was a light drizzle instead of the cold crispness that he was used to. The noises had changed too as they were on a town street instead of muddy country roads.

He sat up as the cart stopped, wondering where he was. It looked as if he was outside a shop with all sorts of strange bottles in the window. An enormous man helped them down from the cart and took them a long way through the shop until they reached a kitchen. Everything looked very strange; he thought he could see a skeleton in one of the rooms until someone shut the door quickly.

Ben thought he was dreaming, and his father was poking the kitchen fire with his usual quick movements. When the man turned after a final flourish, Ben realized that it wasn't his father after all, but he could have been taken for a younger brother.

"Are you my uncle?" he asked.

"Strictly speaking I'm your first cousin once removed," explained Charlie. "But I'm your brother's godfather as well so you can call me Uncle

Charlie."

"Where am I?" asked Ben.

"This is a doctor's surgery," replied Charlie.

"Am I poorly?" asked Ben, remembering all the sour apples.

"Your godfather, Dr. Tom, and I are the doctors who work here. I think you look a bit peaky, so some nice hot tea will warm you up, maybe some bread and jam," said Charlie.

Ben did not think that bread and jam was a good idea.

9 THE FORGE

Tom looked at the two small boys making themselves at home in his kitchen. Dickon was a big strong lad, built like a blacksmith, but sitting very still sipping his tea and ignoring his thick slice of bread and jam. When he looked up he had a strong resemblance to his late grandfather, but without the beard and the extra muscle. His twin brother, little Tommy, had Benjie's wiry build, quick movements, blue eyes and thick black hair. Tommy was obviously getting tired and clumsy, and progressively covered in a thin layer of jam. His drink nearly went flying several times as he fidgeted.

What on earth could have happened at their home, to make them take refuge so far away? How could Benjie be dead? He was a fit man of twenty-seven, not an old man to drop dead suddenly. And how could Nancy be in jail? It must be some misunderstanding; nobody was more honest than Nancy! And couldn't the neighbours have taken the lads in until she came home? But Nipper kept shaking his head, said it might be a long time, he had taken the lads to their kinfolk and now he needed to get back to do his work.

Tom decided that he needed to go to Hilltop, to see if anything could be done for Nancy and to find out whether Benjie's funeral had already taken place. He did not want to delay Nipper; he would set out later on his horse and catch up with the cart on the way. The lads needed to be settled first, and Sally and Susan would know what to do.

***

Tom found the blacksmith's kitchen a lovely peaceful haven in the middle of the uncertainty. Sally was singing as she cleared the breakfast dishes, and he could hear the ringing of metal in the forge. For a moment he hesitated with his news, but he had no excuse to delay and watched Sally's smile fade as she sat down heavily, her dishcloth still in her hands. Kit came in from the forge when he heard the singing stop and he offered to collect the boys right away so that Charlie could get on with his rounds; perhaps he could take them fishing if the rain stopped.

There had been a delay while Sally found a few things for Tom to take to Nancy, but soon the boys were collected and Tom was alone with Charlie in the strangely empty kitchen.

"Did you find out any more?" asked Tom.

"Nipper was in a hurry to go, once the horse had been fed and watered, and I couldn't get a word out of Dickon. I am quite worried about him, he has not spoken since he arrived," said Charlie.

"Young Tommy won't let him have a word in edgeways, I expect," said Tom.

"That must be it, he talked nineteen to the dozen, and he says his name is Ben, not Tommy," said Charlie with a smile and then continued more seriously. "He also says he arrived home to find his father dead, his mother crying about what she had done and Dickon just standing there. He said that the constables took his mother off to jail and he escaped with Dickon before the squire's men could take them to the workhouse. And his mother might be a long time in jail, they didn't usually hang people in Westmorland and what was 'petty treason'?"

"And what did you tell him?" asked Tom.

"I wasn't sure, I thought it was coining," said Charlie, "so I offered him more bread and jam, then he was sick and I have only just finished clearing it up. Dickon just sat there, he must have known what happened but didn't say a word. What is petty treason?"

"When a soldier mutinies, a man kills his master or a woman kills her husband," said Tom, slowly, "surely not. This can't have happened; Ben must be confused. I must go right away, see what can be done."

Charlie reassured him that he could manage the day's work on his own, while Tom repacked his doctor's bag, finding room in the traveling apothecary's chest for the things Sally wanted him to take. There was no way a man of his status would carry a basket.

High on the hill as he got nearer to Hilltop, the problems seemed a long way away. It was a lovely crisp autumn day; the sun was low on the horizon but it was trying to shine. The child's tale seemed very far-fetched, but Nipper was silent and sunk in gloom as he drove his cart; he only spoke to ask if they could go into the town separately so as not to draw attention to themselves.

Joe was pleased to see his brother Tom, but did not know very much about what had happened the previous day. Somehow the squire's family were involved and everyone was being very careful not to upset them as it could make a big difference to their livelihood. Dinner was nearly ready, so Tom decided to eat first and make his way over to the jail afterwards.

One of Joe's colleagues struggled with his dinner as he had toothache, and asked if Tom could pull the tooth out for him afterwards. Nobody was saying much; Tom hoped that the tooth drawing would attract the usual noisy crowd and that they would give away some information.

**

Tom followed directions to the jail that usually housed the local miscreants. The sun shone as he rode down the country lanes; he couldn't believe that life was going on as normal while Nancy's family were suffering such a catastrophe. He saw the barn that doubled as an occasional jail, a ramshackle affair but structurally sound. There were no windows, the place was firmly locked up, and there was no sign of life.

How could they keep his lovely Nancy in a barn like an animal, whatever she had done! The barn looked dirty, cold, and draughty and he thought he saw something going in, something with a tail that looked too big to be a mouse. This was no place for a lady like Nancy, but there was no added unpleasantness like the town jails. At least she would have enough space, and it would be quiet enough to sleep, if sleep was possible.

He called at the farmhouse; the farmer's wife was not very forthcoming but she sent a lad out to fetch her husband from the fields; Tom wondered if he was supervising the potato picking or whether it was too high and cold to grow crops here. The man arrived half an hour later, none too pleased at being disturbed.

"I would like to visit the prisoner, Nancy Armstrong, on behalf of her kinfolk in Cumberland," said Tom.

"You're too late, she's gone," said the farmer.

"Do you know where she went?" asked Tom. His heart leapt at the thought that she might have escaped. But then, how could she have got away without being seen? Perhaps she was hiding locally, and that was why everyone was quiet about her whereabouts. In that case, he should not draw attention to her, and wait to help her get away.

"The squire's men took her, and the constable of course, I didn't ask where. I was glad to get my barn back; it is a nuisance having to house prisoners," said the farmer. "Sorry I can't help you."

"Can you direct me to the squire, so that I can find out where she is?" asked Tom, but the farmer had a strange look on his face.

"I wouldn't go up there asking questions if I were you, it won't help her any. Best let things be," said the farmer, slowly.

"And Benjie Armstrong?" asked Tom, "Do you know when the funeral will be?" Neither Joe nor Nipper had been able to tell him, but said they would let him know as soon as they found out.

"If you mean the carter, he wasn't quite dead but wasn't expected to last long. When the constable got back, he had gone, so someone must have taken him to the infirmary at that new workhouse, God help him! Is that all? I have work to do," said the farmer as he stomped off.

***

Tom wondered why it had been so difficult to get information from the local people; it was like trying to get blood out of a stone. The crowd at the tooth pulling had been strangely quiet;; there were the usual taunts from the two who held the man down but that was all. After it had finished, and the blood was being hosed down from the yard, a messenger arrived asking Tom to call in at the infirmary if he had the time.

Tom was used to the infirmary at home, and expected to find the usual mixture of fevers, old age, childhood ailments and minor wounds. He tried not to hope that Benjie was there, still alive and on the mend; that would bring a quick answer to all their problems. If not, he would have to write to the constabulary through the official channels and hope that he got an answer quickly.

The building was large and forbidding and gloomy. Since parish poorhouses were amalgamated into large workhouses a lot of the humanity seemed to have gone, and the inmates were treated as inconvenient prisoners. The old people seemed very spry and healthy, there was no consumption and typhoid and the few infirmary patients seemed to be suffering from the problems of old age.

There was no sign of Benjie in the men's ward, and nobody had heard of him. In a smaller place, the staff would have known everybody's name and their history. Tom's heart sank as he realized that Benjie must have died on the way, or soon after he arrived. He worked his way through the minor ailments and gave comfort to an old man who had pneumonia and was sinking fast.

Tom was just leaving when he was called back to have a look at a young lad who had been in a fight and had been knocked out. Tom used smelling salts to bring him round, and checked for broken bones.

"You'll live, try and keep out of fights. What was it all about anyway?" asked Tom.

"They said I was a liar! I only said I knew all about the murder and that the prisoner was in the barn," said the lad. Many voices claimed to know different.

"You know nothing!"

"They took her away last night."

"When it was dark."

"Back to her own parish." But Tom knew that was wrong.
"They hurried her off to Kendal for trial."
"Liar! Everyone knows she's going to Carlisle to be hanged."

10 THE LADS

Charlie was glad to sit down after his busy day; Sally was making toast and singing as she worked. Susan was getting the table ready for tea, but he noticed that her face wore a frown when she thought he wasn't watching her. He felt that the forge kitchen was a good place of refuge after a series of patients asking for Dr. Tom, but found it a little quieter than he expected.

"Where are the lads? Out playing with the other children?" asked Charlie, looking for them.

"Dickon wouldn't go, and Tommy didn't want to leave him on his own again. Kit took them out fishing this afternoon, to give them a bit of fresh air," replied Sally.

"They were under our feet all morning," added Susan crossly, "And young Tommy was asking questions all the time, I am surprised that we got any dinner at all."

"I thought the little one liked to be called 'Ben'," said Charlie.

"That's as maybe, but his parents call him Tommy and that is good enough for us. Can't have children picking and choosing their own names," answered Susan.

"They certainly kept us busy," smiled Sally, "but I don't suppose it will be for long. I expect that when Tom comes back he will have everything sorted out and they will be able to go back home."

"I hope so," said Susan, "I wouldn't like either of them to be pupils in my school. Tommy would be a chatterbox, disrupting all the others. Dickon would just sit there like a lump of wood and the other children would pick on him."

"I am sure they'll settle down soon. It'll take a bit of time for them to forget what has happened and start behaving like normal children again.

They must have been badly frightened but it can't be as bad as all that. I am sure Tom will have good news for us when he gets back," replied Sally hopefully.

"I will tell you as soon as I know," answered Charlie, "Tom is expected back late tonight." The toast was being buttered and looked really tempting. Charlie wondered if he could start his tea early.

***

Their peace was shattered by a small whirlwind as the lads arrived. Dickon hesitated in the doorway and remembered to wipe his feet. Ben rushed in, telling about the fish Kit had caught and the brambles that the lads had picked, leaving a large bowl on the table but unpacking his cap and pockets for good measure. Charlie could see that Susan was going to be upset about the mud tracked on to the floor, not to mention the devastating effect of the loose brambles on to the table, there was no way around it. He felt that if he stayed, he might get some of the blame, and he started to make his excuses.

"Sorry, I have to go, the carpenter thinks another of his children is coming down with measles. I am going to be quite busy until Tom gets back," said Charlie.

Susan was marching Ben off to the scullery for a wash, holding him firmly by the ear and scolding him all the time. Kit took in the situation and winked at Dickon, who followed him into the forge.

"Haven't you time to stay for tea?" asked Sally as she put the table to rights, "we made extra toast for you."

"Sorry, must go," answered Charlie, pausing to pick up one or two slices on his way out.

***

Charlie finished his last visit, mended the surgery kitchen fire and made himself something to eat, wishing that he had a little company. He must have dozed off afterwards, for when he woke up the fire was nearly out again, and Tom was sitting at the table with his head in his hands.

"Any news of Benjie?" asked Charlie, but one look at Tom's face made him wish that he hadn't asked.

"I'm so sorry," replied Tom gently.

Charlie sat in silence as he tried to take in the news. Little Ben had said that Benjie was dead, but they had been hoping that the lad was mistaken. Cousin Benjie had been like a protective older brother to Charlie, always looking out for him. It was very hard to believe that he had gone; he must have had a fatal accident, as Benjie always seemed to be in good health.

"Have you any idea what happened?" asked Charlie.

"It was very difficult to find out anything, they all just clammed up as soon as I asked, and seemed afraid of something, or someone," answered Tom, slowly.

"We must pay our respects, Benjie was the only family I had," said Charlie.

"Joe said he would find out about the funeral and let us know," said Tom, "he didn't want me to hang around for some reason. When we get his letter we can make arrangements to go, probably you and Kit if we can't both be spared from the surgery. I never thought there would be another family funeral so soon."

The surgery fire was nearly out, Tom was sitting wearily at the kitchen table and everything seemed very bleak. Charlie hesitated to ask further questions, but there was something he needed to know.

"Did you see Nancy? When does she want her children to go back?" asked Charlie, hoping the situation was not as bad as Ben had said.

"I couldn't find her anywhere, and nobody would tell me anything. There was workhouse gossip about her being sent to Carlisle jail. It seems farfetched but we know she was arrested, and sometimes they send prisoners back to their own county," said Tom. He did not dwell on why she might have been arrested, or why she could have been taken to Carlisle. "I just don't know what to do."

"You should go to Carlisle on the first mail coach, and leave Thunderbolt here rather than take another long ride so soon. Don't worry about the patients, I can manage for another day or two," said Charlie. In happier times he would have reminded Tom that the churchyards were full of indispensable people. "What should I say to Susan and Sally? They were hoping that the lads could go back home soon." Was that a knock on the door, or had he imagined it?

"It's best to say as little as possible. We won't know anything for sure until I have seen Nancy, there might still be a reasonable explanation. We have no proof of Benjie's death and don't want to upset the lads unnecessarily. Just ask Sally and Susan to look after the boys for a bit longer, potato picking week is coming up so there'll be no school. I expect they're getting quite attached to the youngsters; women usually do." said Tom.

Charlie tried to keep his face straight as he remembered the last time he saw Susan with Ben; no signs of attachment there. He realized that the request to look after the children might not be popular, as Susan usually liked to put her feet up during the school holidays, and there were the cottages to see to as well. The knocking was getting louder; he couldn't ignore it any longer.

"Sounds like someone needs a doctor. I'll go this time, Tom, you get some rest," said Charlie.

***

Charlie was still regretting his generosity twenty-four hours later; it looked like another long night at Mrs. Jepson's. Her granddaughter was sleeping fitfully in the bed the women usually shared, and there had been no improvement in spite of all Charlie's efforts to bring the fever down. Measles could strike anybody at any time, but he thought that in this case it was very unfair.

Rebecca Jepson was a promising pupil at the school, due to start work in the mill at the end of term. She had previously been lined up as the next pupil teacher, but her father's sudden death meant that she had to be breadwinner sooner rather than later if she and her grandmother were to avoid the workhouse. Both women took in plain sewing, but the income would not be enough to keep them for long and Rebecca could earn a good wage at the mill. Now it looked as if Rebecca would not last the night, and all their contriving was in vain. Mrs. Jepson would watch the last of her family die before she took the final humiliating step to the workhouse.

Charlie wearily mused on the shortness of childhood; the responsibilities of an adult came all too quickly. He supposed that he had been relatively lucky himself, taken from the poorhouse to be a surgeon's apprentice at the age of twelve. A short time ago he had been a relatively carefree journeyman, but now he was doing a full man's job. Charlie had always wondered why the grownups were so miserable; he now knew that they were too tired to enjoy themselves. He could see his patient fading away in front of his eyes, in spite of his best efforts and he knew that a measles epidemic would run its course every few years. Some patients survived but too many died, and some were left impaired in movement, senses or understanding.

Charlie had been able to call in briefly at the forge, to let them know that they would have to wait a bit longer for any news. Susan did not take too kindly to his message, her bad temper in stark contrast to Sally's tears. Different people had their ways of coping, Susan was hiding herself in activity and everyone else was pussyfooting around her. The main bone of contention was a muslin bag full of brambles, tied to an upturned stool as the juice strained into a bowl. The contraption looked precarious, and much too near the door – Ben had already upset it twice and Kit once before the door slammed into it again. Charlie had made his excuses to go, saying that he was run off is feet. He smiled at the memory, but he had been glad not to be asked any more questions.

Suddenly he noticed that there had been a change in his patient, Rebecca was breathing more easily now and seemed to be sleeping normally. He got up to draw back the rag that served for a curtain so that he could see more clearly. The room contained a bed, a coffer and a chair; there had been a rug at one time but it must have been sold with the china. Charlie stood for a minute or two to admire the magnificent sunrise, thinking that there could not be much wrong with the world when he could see such a wonderful sky. Time to tell Mrs. Jepson the good news; she was so worn out that she had fallen asleep in the chair.

Mrs. Jepson was overjoyed to see her granddaughter's recovery, but Charlie was still a bit anxious in case Rebecca had been left with permanent problems.

"Oh, grandma, I had such a strange dream. There was mother, father, Annie and the baby all welcoming me back to the house we used to live in, but I knew I had to come back to you. Have I missed dinner? I'm really hungry," said Rebecca.

"It's wonderful that you are back with us," said Mrs. Jepson. "I was so worried."

"It looks as if my favourite patient has made a full recovery," said Charlie.

"You say that to all the girls!" said Rebecca. "Could somebody open the curtain – it's very dark in here."

Half an hour later, Charlie realized that Rebecca had survived with her hearing and wits intact but lost most of her sight. This was the worst possible case, as there was work for the deaf and the simple but the blind had no alternative but the workhouse.

11 THE PRISONER

After a long and fruitless day questioning officials at the Carlisle jail, Tom decided to call on his sister Mary Ann and see if her landlady, Mrs. McKay, had a room for the night. It was too late to go back home that day, and he hoped to go back and get some further information the next day, hoping that different staff might be on duty.

He couldn't believe the difference in his little sister since she left home to become a milliner in the big city. She called herself 'Marianne', and sprinkled little French phrases into her conversation about family news; she thought it would be good for business, but Tom thought she was just showing off.

They sat in Mrs. McKay's front room, regaled with tea and tiny sandwiches and dainties. The minute mouthfuls contrasted with the thick slices of good honest toast at the forge. Tom thought it must be very difficult to get used to city ways. In his hometown, people who had front rooms never used them, even if they managed to furnish them, but in Carlisle things seemed to be very different. The large window had a pair of matching curtains and there was a large square of drugget spread over the flags. There were more chairs than people, several superfluous little tables with ornaments on them and gaslights on the walls. Tom did not want to talk much about the real reason for his visit, as it would be too painful. Mary Ann, however, was genuinely concerned for her friends Susan and Sally and she liked to keep up with all the news.

"And they couldn't give you any indication why Nancy had been taken? Or where she is now?" asked Mary Ann.

"They said they'd never heard of her," answered Tom gloomily. He was glad to see that Mary Ann was beginning to drop the French phrases, but did not really want to talk about what was happening to Nancy.

"What are you going to do next?" asked Mary Ann, "You can't just go home without finding out. Poor Sally and Susan must be really worried."

"It is very difficult to find out whether people aren't telling you, or genuinely don't know. I will try the jail again tomorrow, perhaps someone will have records somewhere," said Tom.

"Perhaps my son Henry can help you," said Mrs. McKay as she poured the tea, "he has a very important job with the newspaper and they get to know everything."

Mary Ann rushed off eagerly to fetch this wonderful personage, who turned out to be a stocky bespectacled youth very much dazzled by Mary Ann. Tom felt a bit strange, as he thought that he was always going to be the most important man in the family, but felt better when he found out that Henry did not edit the paper or gather news; as a printer compositor he just arranged letters in a frame for printing.

Henry was good-natured enough, and invited Tom to the newspaper office the next day, as he was sure that Tom would be interested in the machinery. The women said they were sorry they would not be able to go; they had obviously seen it all before. Watching Henry with his mother, Tom decided that Mary Ann (or whatever she called herself) could do a lot worse, and he hoped that Henry's intentions were honourable.

***

The next day Tom was at the newspaper office, trying to look interested in all the machinery that Henry was showing him. Henry's enthusiasm was normally infectious, but Tom was still preoccupied, having again drawn a blank at the jail that morning. He found Henry looking at him, expecting an answer, and had to think quickly.

"Ingenious bit of machinery you have there; it looks very complicated and it must be very difficult to get the letters right."

"Yes, but I've got used to it, I'll show you again, you just…"

"There don't seem many people here, considering. Who does the writing?"

"There are two reporters, and a lad who is learning the trade. We have an artist who draws pictures and the editor (that's our boss) tells everyone what to do and checks our work."

"Where are they all? Out on a big story somewhere?"

"They will be sending the artist and a reporter to Whitehaven for two or three days. It is quite a performance getting them on to the mail coach with their luggage. The editor says he needs to see them off to make sure they don't skive and make the stories up afterwards. The other lads go to see them off because sometimes mail coach passengers have to come off to make room for the newspaper folk, and they don't always take too kindly. If there are a few of us there they don't argue so much."

"Why are they going to Whitehaven?"

"To report the trials at the assizes, and they usually stay for the hangings as well. I'm glad I don't have to do it but it sells newspapers and keeps us in work."

"Are Carlisle people really interested in Whitehaven trials?"

"Quite often the local bad lads are sent to Whitehaven if the 'powers that be' want a quick trial and sentence. Their assizes come up before ours and it makes for less overcrowding in the jail. Handy for transportations too, as sometimes prisoners are marched from the dock straight to the ships."

Tom shuddered. "When are the next assizes?" he asked.

"Tomorrow," answered Henry.

***

It was two days before Tom could get a place on the mail coach to Whitehaven, and even then he had to ride on top with the luggage; he did not mind an uncomfortable ride if only he got there on time. The coach jolted over the uneven roads and Tom clung on grimly; he would have liked the coach to go faster but not if it meant falling off.

The roughness of the ride only partially distracted Tom from his thoughts. Was he on a wild goose chase because Nancy had been taken somewhere else, back to Carlisle or had never been there in the first place? There was no proof that she had even been to Carlisle, but where else could she have gone? Suppose he got to the jail but it was already too late and the sentence had been carried out? If he hadn't dithered he would have got there earlier, but he hesitated to leave Charlie on his own too long with the measles epidemic. It was Mary Ann who convinced him, repacking his bags and telling him to hurry.

Night was falling when he arrived; he dithered again but decided to leave one of his bags at the coaching Inn before he looked for the jail. It was a depressing building, strongly built but providing no comfort, even bleaker than the new workhouses. The jailer was old and tired, with a world-weary expression; he had obviously seen it all.

"Have you a prisoner called Nancy Armstrong," asked Tom.

The jailer got down a very dog-eared book and tried to make out the words.

"Tall, generously built, well spoken, not from round here?" asked Tom, trying to jog his memory.

"Oh yes, I remember now. She is the only one in the women's room now. There were two local women accused of stealing but they got away with it. They were sent home with a warning but I expect I'll see them again," answered the jailer.

Tom did not know whether to be glad or sorry that he had finally found Nancy; the fact that she had obviously had her trial but was still imprisoned did not bode well. He wondered how long her jail sentence would be, and whether he could do anything to make it more comfortable.

"Can I see Mrs. Armstrong?" asked Tom.

"It is too late for visitors tonight, most of the guards have gone home," said the jailer. "You have plenty of time to see the murderess before they hang her on Friday."

***

Tom caught a glimpse of Nancy before she saw him; she looked tired, despondent, as if she had given up on life already. The bare cell had no furniture so she had spread her cloak on the floor to make a bed. The only light was through a small barred window in the thick wall, and Tom could see writing materials there. Nancy must have been standing there, he thought, the only place she could see to write.

What a terrible place to be, solitary, no comfort, not a place to contemplate a grim future. It was very cold, no sun through the window, it must be deadly in the depth of winter. Tom did not know what to say; he did not like to ask what happened, and what was about to happen loomed over them. Charlie would have asked, Susan definitely would have asked, but Tom hesitated. He wanted to just take her in his arms and make everything all right, but he knew that was impossible. Nancy saw him, drew herself up to her full height, stepped towards him and took charge.

"Are the children all right? I can't remember them being in the yard when the constable took me. I can't bear to think of them all alone out in the open somewhere," said Nancy. "If they have been taken to the workhouse, you must release them and bring them up – as godfather it is your duty. If they are lost, you must find them and give them a home."

"The boys are safe," said Tom. "I am more worried about you; why are you here? I can get a lawyer to fight your case and set you free..."

"Where are they? Who is looking after them?"

"They are at the forge for now. But ..."

"I am beyond help. What do you mean 'for now'? You can't send them back to Hilltop, they can't go to the workhouse, and you must look after them. Are they all right?"

"The lads have settled in nicely at the forge." He did not say anything about Ben annoying Susan, or that Dickon had not spoken since he arrived. "Charlie and I have an epidemic on our hands, so the boys are better where they are for the moment. Surely we can appeal against the sentence, I can't believe what they say about you; there must be some mistake."

Nancy was in floods of tears by now, but they were tears of relief that her boys would be safe. Tom waited for her to compose herself; if she did not want to talk about what happened, he would not press her.

"There's no mistake," said Nancy slowly, "I have been tried and sentenced, and they made sure that there would be no time for an appeal. I am happy to die for what I have done. I don't want to live now Benjie is dead."

"Are you sure there is nothing that can be done?"

"Nothing anyone can do, ever again." said Nancy. She continued, very quietly, "Benjie was late and I knew that he was with Milady again, so I went to fetch him home - I found them in the hayloft. She was there with a big smile on her face and her dress buttoned up all wrong. I wanted to box her ears but the squire was…"

They were interrupted by the arrival of the priest, so Tom had to wait for a while before he was allowed back in.

***

Nancy was composed and imperious when Tom saw her again, and neither of them broached the subject of the murder or the hanging. Nancy had finished her writing, and had an envelope in her hand.

"Take this letter, the boys are to read it when they are much older, preferably twenty-one. I want them to have this cloak; I will have it sent to you tomorrow, as I will need it tonight. Go now, on the next mail coach," said Nancy.

"I would like to stay, you should have someone of your own in this god forsaken place," said Tom.

"I need to keep my dignity, and I will just go to pieces if anyone is kind to me. Just go, or I will call the jailer – he will send you out and not allow you to visit," said Nancy. "Don't touch me, I can't bear it."

12 THE MYSTERY

Charlie was coping as best he could with the extra work, and wondering what was keeping Tom in Carlisle. His time was spent visiting patients and quite often he did not finish until late. Then he had to go to the ale house to patch men up after the fights, so that the patients could be taken home in the wheelbarrow without making too much mess.

He did not have many opportunities to open the shop; he worried about this because that was where they made most of their money. He could have done with the loan of a lad to sit in the shop and take messages, but Susan said the boys were too young and unreliable and would not help him out.

He spoke to Arthur and they came up with the idea of Charlie trading from the ale house, with Arthur's staff taking messages during the day and Charlie bringing the orders in the late evening. This worked well except that Susan realized that Charlie had very little time to visit her, but people could always find him at the ale house. The last time at the forge he was reminded (loudly) where his responsibilities lay, and where he should be spending his time.

Charlie knew that Susan was anxious about Nancy, and was finding the boys hard work, and that the situation was getting more and more difficult as the week wore on. He had less and less success in using his charm, and stopped going to the forge. This did not suit Susan either; she wanted him there to be shouted at.

They both assumed that Benjie was dead, but what would happen if Nancy never came back? This Charlie could not say, even if he could have got a word in edgeways, and he had the additional worry of what would happen if Tom never came back.

***

Charlie was very relieved to see Tom, early on Friday evening, but had not realized how bad his news was going to be. After he had got over the shock, and the unfairness, he thought of one or two questions he wanted to ask.

"Did you ask Nancy to tell you exactly how it happened, and whether the children were there?"

"Benjie was the love of her life, she feels that she is responsible for his death and she has been convicted of murder. I just couldn't ask her for the details; she is suffering enough."

"Even if it was an accident?"

"It must have been an accident, but even then I just couldn't bring myself to ask her."

"So we'll never know?"

"It will probably be in this letter she gave me; the boys are to read it when they are older."

"Why didn't you say so before? Let's get the kettle on, we can steam the letter open right away." Charlie started filling the kettle. "After we seal it up again, nobody will ever know."

"I can't do that, I can't read a letter addressed to someone else without their permission," said Tom, "anyway when did you learn to steam open letters?"

"I can't remember, I must have always known," said Charlie quickly. He realized that Tom did not really want to hear the details of what happened, but other people needed to be informed. "What do we tell Susan and Sally? They deserve to know the truth."

"We will tell them all we know; perhaps there will be a letter for them with the cloak."

"And the children? We can't tell them their mother was hanged! Not yet, they are too young, although we can't contradict anything they have already seen."

"There was a terrible accident which resulted in the death of both their parents," answered Tom, slowly.

Charlie wanted to know how his cousin had died, and he had one last question.

"Is Henry sending us the newspaper with the account of the trial in it? He must be able to get spare copies."

"I never thought. At the time I wasn't even sure she was at Whitehaven, and I came straight back here afterwards. I suppose I could write and ask if you really want."

If Charlie had realized at the time that there would be no communication from Whitehaven or Carlisle, he would have made sure by writing the letter himself.

***

Charlie went to the forge later that evening to break the news, which came as a shock to all concerned. Sally was weeping in Kit's arms and Susan was bustling about noisily, while Charlie tried to think about the practicalities. He thought that it was very hard on the family, losing their father, sister and brother-in-law within a week – he wanted to help all he could but Susan did not always make it easy.

"Tom says that he'll set up an account in one of the drapers for you, and to let him know about any more money that you need," said Charlie.

"Just how long do you expect us to look after your godchildren for?" asked Susan. "They should be your responsibility."

"They are young, they still need a woman's loving care," said Charlie, who had been orphaned early and fended for himself for a while before going to the poorhouse.

"They are no bother," said Kit. "Sleeping upstairs like angels without a care in the world." Susan bristled indignantly.

"We can't look after them now," said Charlie. "Tom and I have to go out to patients at night, we can't do that and look after little children sleeping at home. We have to earn a living; of course we can contribute more money for their food."

"They came with only the clothes they stood up in," said Susan, "absolutely destitute. Is there anything to come from the carting business at Hilltop? Father gave Benjie a good horse and cart when they got married."

"Tom said something about their goods being seized, I am not sure, maybe I can find out from Joe. The only thing Tom mentioned was that Nancy was arranging for her cloak to be sent. I don't see what use that will be," said Charlie.

The thought of Nancy set Sally off crying again, which wasn't helpful.

"A cloak is always useful, good warm fabric. It could be a blanket for a bed or cut down for other clothes," said Susan thoughtfully.

"Nancy sewed mother's jewellery into the hem of that cloak," sobbed Sally, "it was the last thing she did before she went back. To think that those poor little orphans could be in the workhouse now without a friend in the world, if Joe hadn't sent them back here."

"Of course we'll look after them," soothed Kit, "What else could we do? We'll manage somehow."

"I know it will be difficult with two more mouths to feed, but we can help with the expense," said Charlie.

"It isn't just the money, it is all the time and the work and the aggravation," grumbled Susan. "Tommy is particularly hard work, I have hardly had a minute to myself this week. And next week I will have to teach them all day in school and look after them when they get home, I'm not looking forward to it at all."

Charlie was puzzled; he thought that all women loved looking after children. "Maybe we need to hire someone to do the washing and the heavy cleaning, I will talk to Tom."

"I am sure we can manage…" said Sally.

"I think we need a talk tomorrow evening, with Tom here as well, before we decide anything," said Susan.

"When you look at their little sleeping faces, don't you think it's all worth it?" asked Sally. Kit held her close and gave her a kiss but Susan just looked at her in amazement.

13 THE SILENCE

Susan did not think that the talk on the boys' future had gone the way she wanted it to. Why did everyone think that women actually liked looking after children, or looking after anyone for that matter? Why did men think that women would have enough time and energy to look after children, especially the awkward ones? Susan left work with little voices ringing in her ears and looked forward to the silence when she came home.

She enjoyed teaching new skills to keen youngsters; it was just the day-to-day care that was a chore. Making sure that feet and noses were wiped, and that children were not too much of a danger to themselves and each other. And all those chattering voices in the playground; she was the only teacher that insisted on silence in the classroom. There would be no escape now; other people's children would always surround her. She realized a terrible misfortune had befallen Nancy, but wondered if her sister had met it half way with her irresponsibility. Now her sisters had to pick up the pieces.

Sally was in the forge, talking to Kit, but Susan lingered at the table with her cup of tea, enjoying the quiet while the boys made their beds and tidied their room. Soon there would be the clatter of feet on the stairs, and she was making the most of time to herself.

"I think there may be something wrong with Dickon," wondered Sally as she came in, "Kit can't get a word out of him."

"We will see about that," said Susan. "I can always get small boys to talk."

She held out two apples as the boys came down, and asked if they would like one before they went out to play. Although Tommy said, "Yes, please!" and took his apple, Dickon held back.

"Would you like an apple, Dickon?" asked Susan, although she had begun to wonder whether all the unwelcome children's chatter was coming from just one voice. Dickon stood there hopefully and nodded his head.

"You must speak to me before you get your apple, and stop playing games," said Susan, in the voice that was always obeyed when she was teaching her class. Dickon mouthed something but no sound came.

"I am still waiting," said Susan.

Tommy gave Dickon his own apple and rushed out to play, dodging the clip round the ear that he knew he deserved.

***

Now that Susan admitted that there was a problem, she tried all day to make Dickon speak, and she was infuriated when his brother spoke for him. Had Nancy landed them with an idiot child as well as a troublesome one? She decided to send Tommy to bed at the usual time, but kept Dickon up later so that the doctors could see him before the family conference that evening.

Susan and Sally were kept busy with the problem of the children's clothes; neither of them had made breeches before and did not know where to start. They enlisted the help of Tom's sister-in-law Jeannie, who had been a dressmaker in her younger days; her son Jack was the same age as the twins. They had hoped that Jeannie would do the work for them but she was far too busy looking after George and the children: Jack, his younger sister Deborah and the new baby.

Jeannie's little house used to be as neat as a new pin, but now it was cluttered with children's clothes and toys. All the time they were there Jack was running in and out, and he seemed very full of himself. Deborah was whining and the baby lay grizzling in the cradle, which Jeannie rocked with her foot while she prepared vegetables for dinner. Susan did not think this boded well, but she took over peeling the potatoes and Sally picked up the baby, leaving Jeannie free to give them the benefit of her experience in making all sorts of clothes.

Jeannie helped them make a list of what they would need, and explained how to cut out and put together the problem breeches so they could make a start on the tedious work. Susan sat and sewed all afternoon, when she would have liked to get on with more interesting things, and was becoming more and more resentful of her burden. It was all right for Sally, she would be free of the children during the day, but it looked as if the children would be in Susan's class as well as being underfoot in the evenings.

***

Neither doctor could find anything physically wrong with Dickon, but he did not seem to be able to speak to them. When he was in bed, and they had checked to see that neither of the boys was listening, they spoke about the problem for the first time.

"Did Nancy say that the boy was mute, or that his wits were addled?" asked Charlie.

"According to his brother, Dickon can read, write and reckon a bit and never got into trouble at school. Apparently he could speak, but I don't suppose he got a word in very often," replied Sally.

"I have heard of people being struck dumb after a shock," said Tom slowly, "but I never came across a case before."

"Do you think that's what happened?" asked Charlie, "Perhaps he just doesn't want to talk about anything he saw that day. If he went straight home from school, wasn't kept in at school and didn't go out to play, he must have been there when…"

Tom silenced him with a look.

"If he's suffering from shock, I'm not sure when he will recover. He may never speak again," said Tom gloomily. "I am not sure what is best to be done."

"He certainly can't attend school," said Susan, "the other children will pick on him unmercifully, especially as he's not from round here. I can't be looking out for him all the time because I have a job to do."

"Couldn't he just go into the infant class like the simpleton did?" asked Sally.

"It's not just that, I don't see how education would benefit him. What work could he do in the future? The simpleton found work scaring birds but Dickon won't even be able to do that!" said Susan.

"Are you saying that there would be no place in the school for him?" asked Charlie.

"I suppose I am. Life is hard enough for those that can work for a living and we won't always be here to look after him. And that brother of his looks as if he was born to be …" said Susan, "but maybe we can beat it out of him. I am very sorry but Dickon belongs in the workhouse."

"The lad could recover," said Tom.

"It looks unlikely," replied Susan sharply.

"The poor lad is witness to a terrible tragedy, and has just lost his parents and his home. Give him a chance! We would be taking away a second home and his brother," said Sally, her eyes filling with tears again.

"It would be kinder in the long run," said Susan, "He certainly can't go to school, and the workhouse is the only place in this town for a mouth that cannot feed itself."

"Perhaps we could wait a little while and see if he recovers," said Charlie, "you never know."

"He would have nothing to do all day and be under Sally's feet," said Susan.

"Just for a while, I need to find out whether they would take him at the local workhouse as he wasn't born in the parish," said Charlie, "perhaps Kit has a few odd jobs for him in the forge."

"He is a big strong lad, good at fetching and carrying, and has nearly got the hang of the bellows," said Kit, looking at Sally. "I am sure I can keep him busy. Your father gave me a chance when I needed it. And Dr. Tom gave Charlie a chance."

"Just for a while, then," said Susan, "as Kit is much too busy to look after an idiot child all day." She had a suspicion that Charlie would 'keep forgetting' to ask about the workhouse unless she kept reminding him, but the current arrangement would keep Sally happy.

14 THE NEW SCHOOL

The following Monday, trailing behind his Aunt Susan, Ben set off very reluctantly for his new school. Why wasn't he allowed to stay and play with his brother, like he wanted? It just wasn't fair, but when he argued he just got a clip round the ear and was told to hurry up. His new clothes were very uncomfortable, the collar chafed and his new breeches were far too big. He had been told he would grow into them but he was sure that would not happen in a month of Sundays and the other children would laugh at him. Ben saw a large conker tree and slowed down to have a look, and see if it was going to be easy to climb.

"Hurry up, Tommy, don't dawdle, you have made us late enough as it is," said Aunt Susan.

It was a while before he realized that she was talking to him, he had explained to everyone that his name was 'Ben'; but Aunt Susan never seemed to listen. Instead she had grabbed him by the hand and was yanking him along. Ben was worrying about his brother; what would happen to Dickon when Ben wasn't at home to speak for him? Another pull on his arm made him hurry, but what would the other children think if they saw him holding teacher's hand like a baby. Ben needn't have worried; by the time they arrived at the school he was being firmly held by the ear.

***

It was school, and yet it wasn't. It was far too big with three large classrooms and he didn't know anybody. Everything was in the wrong place, the wrong pictures on the walls and rows and rows of desks; the children had to even ask permission to move. His class was in was a very long room, with three long columns of two-seater benches; each place had a writing desk in front with a shelf underneath. Ben thought that it would be impossible to hide untidiness, or anything else, in desks as open as that.

He sat in the middle of the middle column, and felt as if everyone was looking at him, as all the other children seemed to be in pairs. There was a window high up at the back of the class, but the children could not see out without climbing on the back row of desks and he did not think that would be allowed. Aunt Susan's desk stood between an unlit fire on the right and a door to the other classrooms on the left.

There was a playground outside, in front of the school, and a path to the schoolhouse and its small garden at the back. This looked promising as the playground had a large pile of coal near the privies; it would be really good to slide down the pile of coal, and he wondered if playtime would be soon. He heard a voice in the background calling some child named 'Tommy' to pay attention and wondered why the child didn't answer.

"I think you had better move desks, so I can keep an eye on you," said Aunt Susan as she loomed over him. She marched him over to an empty desk in the front row, right in front of her own desk. Ben felt that she could almost reach his knuckles with the ruler without getting up from her chair.

"Why didn't you answer me?" she asked sternly.

"I didn't know you meant me, Auntie, as my name is 'Ben'," he said.

"You call me 'Miss Graham', like the other children do," said Aunt Susan. Ben could hear the children laughing; how could he have made such a silly mistake as to call her 'Auntie' instead of 'Miss'. "And you can stay in at playtime for answering back." She continued. "All children must open their reading books, and that includes you."

"I haven't got one, Miss," said Ben, and Aunt Susan took a book from a pile and slammed it on to his desk.

"You will all read to me in turn starting from page twenty," said Aunt Susan, pointing at a boy in the corner who looked like his friend Johnny Harrison.

Ben had not seen the reading book before, but turned to page 20 to follow the words so that he was ready when his turn came. However, some of the progress was very slow and he found himself reading on ahead for the rest of the story. After he got to the end, he took a look at the beginning bit that he had missed and by the time his turn came he had no idea where in the book he was supposed to be.

"Your turn now, Tommy," said Aunt Susan, "start where Deborah has just finished reading."

Ben frantically looked through the book for the words that Deborah had just read, and couldn't find them anywhere.

"You haven't bothered to listen," shouted Aunt Susan, "stand in that corner for the rest of the morning. And you lose your playtime after dinner."

***

Ben got more despondent as the week wore on; he was always kept in at playtime, and the coal was cleared away from the yard before he got a chance to play on it. On one awful day the whole class was kept in because of something he had done, and the other children wouldn't speak to him for a while. He won them round by pulling faces and telling jokes, which earned him more time in the corner. In his old school he hadn't been expected to read out loud like the babies; there was a pile of exciting books at the back of the class for the better readers to read quietly.

Aunt Sally had told him that Aunt Susan had to be strict with him so he would not look as if he was a favourite, but Ben would not have minded being teacher's pet occasionally for a change. Dickon was all right, he liked helping Uncle Kit in the forge- all the grownups said that he was proving to be very useful (not like some!).

The class was reading aloud again, and Ben was distracted by one of the pictures on the wall. This picture was very interesting because it showed the names of all the wild plants and had something interesting to say about all of them, and it had his full attention. All too soon it was Ben's turn to read and he had lost his place again. He sighed, got up, hung his head and set off for the corner that he had made his own; pausing by Aunt Susan's desk with his knuckles held out for the ruler.

"You don't get off so easily this time," said Aunt Susan, sternly. "See Mr. Corrie at the end of the afternoon."

"Will he get the cane, miss?" asked one of older girls.

"Very probably," answered Aunt Susan, "now let that be a lesson to all of you."

The children looked impressed, some of the little girls started to cry, and Ben felt very brave. He bowed to the class and received some applause from the older boys.

***

Later on that afternoon, standing last in a queue of bigger boys, he did not feel brave at all. The classroom was a mirror image of his own, which seemed very strange, and he tried not to think about what was about to happen. Each boy was given a lecture on his behaviour, received one or more cane strokes on each of his outstretched hands, and was sent home. Ben shuffled into place, holding his hands in front of him as he had seen the other boys do, and holding his tears back. There was a silence as Ben waited for the tall, imposing headmaster to speak.

"You have not made a very good start, lad," said Mr. Corrie.

"No, sir," said Ben.

"Miss Graham says you have made no attempt at all to learn to read and write."

"Sorry, sir."

"If you are unlettered when you leave this school there will be no apprenticeship and nobody will give you regular work. If you cannot pay attention to instructions you will not have any sort of a job, and you will starve or go to the workhouse. Do you understand me?"

"Yes, sir." Ben stretched out his hands in front of him and tried to wait for the blows without flinching. To help himself he stared at a picture on the wall, very similar to the one in his own matching classroom but with wild animals instead of plants. There was a very interesting bit about rabbits and how they lived, and it helped him deal with the two strokes of the cane he received. He stood and waited for the next stroke, interesting himself in the habits of squirrels; he must look out for them, as there had been none at home. Ben did not notice that Mr. Corrie had put his cane away and was standing looking at him.

"Pay attention, lad. What is so fascinating about that picture?" asked Mr. Corrie.

"Squirrels, sir. I know about rabbits because I used to help my dad bring one home for the pot but I have never seen a squirrel, sir."

"Look carefully in the treetops as you go home, there might be one or two. You obviously weren't paying attention before."

"It says on the picture that squirrels like woods and yours are much better than the ones at home, sir."

Mr. Corrie asked him to read the words on the picture, which he found easy.

"You can read this chart, so why couldn't you read your book when Miss Graham asked you?"

"I tried to keep my place, but the children were so slow, and there were so many. I read a bit more of the story while I was waiting and then I lost my place, sir."

"Can you write your name on this slate, lad?"

Ben wrote his name carefully in joined up writing, and handed the slate to Mr. Corrie.

"I thought your name was 'Tommy'."

"My name is 'Ben', sir. 'Benjamin Thomas', in full and I'm proud to have my grandfather's name." And my father's, Ben thought sadly. "Sometimes people call me 'Tommy' and I don't realize they mean me."

"And why couldn't you write for Miss Graham, lad?"

"I wanted to do it right. Miss Graham likes the children to print, so I tried to do it like the others and not do joined up writing. But I kept forgetting and it came out a bit of a muddle and then I forgot where I was, sir."

"Miss Graham said that she hadn't had any work out of you all week,

Ben. I expect you spent a lot of time standing in the corner. You had better start working now to make up for lost time."

Ben had to do quite a lot of arithmetic, copy and learn a poem, turn away from the picture and answer questions about the animals. He felt that he had never worked so hard in his life and it felt surprisingly good. Mr. Corrie gave him a talk on working hard, paying attention, behaving well and then said he could go home.

15 THE RESPONSIBILITIES

Susan rearranged her classroom cupboards, irritated to be kept waiting by her nephew. She found more and more things that were not to her liking, including various objects that had been taking space in her classroom since Nancy's time as a teacher, and decided that they should all go. Susan was making too much noise to hear what was going on in the next classroom; it was taking a long time but would be worth it if her nephew were suitably chastened.

Two of Mr. Corrie's class were to start work at the mill the next Monday, and her two best scholars were due to be promoted to the top class. She had dropped a few hints during the week; Jack Harrison and his friend Sam Brown were looking forward to joining the big boys. Susan just hoped that Elizabeth would not be sending too many of her mewling infants to replace them as young Tommy was keeping her busy.

The door opened and Mr. Corrie emerged with the offending child, who seemed to be almost smiling. She briskly sent him to collect his coat, and Mr. Corrie suggested that the lad might hear better if she called him 'Ben' instead of 'Tommy'. This did not help her temper any as the two of them set off home for a belated tea.

***

Everything seemed well at the forge, and Susan's irritation evaporated in the face of Sally's good humour. When the boys had gone to bed and Kit was finishing some work in the forge, Sally was mending some stockings while Susan tried to think of work to set her class the following week.

"Kit is really pleased with the way young Dickon is turning out," Sally put down her mending with a happy smile.

"Is he finding little jobs for him to do, or is he under his feet all the time?"

"Dickon is really useful, fetching and carrying and seeing to the horses. He can even work the bellows; it usually takes new lads a while to get the hang of it."

"Has Dickon enough wit to understand what he is supposed to do? He could be a danger to himself and others."

"He understands well enough," said Kit as he came in with Charlie, "and the lack of chatter is quite refreshing. Talking of refreshment…"

"It is all right to find odd jobs for a small boy," said Susan, as Sally handed tankards of beer to the men, "but will Dickon ever be able to earn his own living?" It was one thing looking after children for three or four years until they started work, but what if they were incapable of earning their own bread? Would their relatives have to be responsible for them forever?

"He will be fit to start as my apprentice in four years' time," said Kit, "then he will always have a trade. As he is, he could even make journeyman; if he ever speaks again he could go further."

"But he will be unschooled," said Susan.

"It never did me any harm," said Kit.

"I am sure I could teach him to write his name, and reckon a little, "said Sally, "Surely a schoolteacher's son has some idea."

"You would think so," said Susan, "but they come from a village, and don't have our advantages. Young Tommy has made no attempt to read or write all week, and doesn't take instruction well. I just don't know what will happen to him."

"Adam Corrie said he had a word with young Ben," said Charlie, with a smile, remembering his own schooldays. "I am sure he will settle in time; small boys often need correction."

"But what if he doesn't settle?" asked Susan, "How will he earn his bread?" She felt that Charlie, like most men, was being impractical. This was worrying, and something she needed to sort out before their marriage.

"It seems that my godson's future is settled," replied Charlie, "and if Ben does not settle down and improve in a year or two, I am sure that Dr Tom will take some responsibility for his. Stop worrying, I am sure that the boys will be fine."

***

It is all right for Charlie to tell her to stop worrying, thought Susan as the children filed into her classroom. It was all right for him to say that everything usually sorted itself out, but it didn't sort itself out for everybody. Blinking back the tears, she tried not to think about Nancy; things were never going to sort themselves out for her. Susan did not want to rely on 'things sorting themselves out' as she preferred to have a good grip on everything so that life had no surprises. Everything in her world should be firmly under her control, including her awkward nephew if he was not to suffer the same fate as his parents. She blinked back her tears again.

She could hear the infants next door; they were obviously unsettled, wondering who would be moving up to the next class- some had obviously started snivelling in the hope that they would not be chosen. Her own class found their desks and waited excitedly, knowing that something was about to happen. Jack Harrison and his friend Sam were expecting promotion and secretly getting their things together, very proud of themselves.

Susan indicated silence, and started the day with the usual prayers, and the children stopped fidgeting. In the silence afterwards she added her own prayers for her life to go back to normal. She could not ask for a large miracle, like the return of Nancy and Benjie; that was too much to expect of a God who could not turn the clock back and had many other things to do. But a small miracle like taking her irritating nephew off her hands – perhaps Charlie's friend at the workhouse could take him in for a week or so and frighten him a little. Or maybe Dr. Tom could do his share when the measles epidemic was over, but Dr. Tom could be irresponsible and was not setting Charlie a good example. Or God could magic some other relatives out of nowhere, really keen to give the lads a home.

Susan knew that most women, including Sally, grew fond of the children that they were looking after, and wondered if she was unnatural. Children were all right, mostly; she could manage being surrounded by them all day (just) but she wondered what the fuss was about.

"Mr. Corrie will be here soon, and he may have some news for the two best scholars," said Susan, watching Jack and Sam preen themselves a little. "Children who work hard and behave themselves will always get their reward. Open your reading books, please, and read aloud in turn, starting with Jack."

Susan listened to Jack reading from the back of the class, loud, clear and fluent; he was a credit to her teaching. She hoped that Mr. Corrie would come in soon, and hear the better readers. If he were late he would hear younger children stumbling over their words, or the daily tussle trying to get her nephew's attention. She was in luck; Sam was reading shortly afterwards when the door opened.

"Good work, Sam!" praised Adam. "Miss Graham, I have come for two of your pupils for my class, Jack Harrison and Ben Armstrong." Jack efficiently picked up his books, but Ben was frantically grabbing and dropping his things as he made ready to go before Mr. Corrie changed his mind.

"Are you sure?" asked Susan, watching Sam's crestfallen face with wobbly lower lip. "Tommy has only been here a week and is nowhere near your standard."

"Ben will be fine, but will have to work a bit harder," said Adam. "Sorry, Sam, I only have two places at the moment." He went back to his classroom followed by two eager boys and one or two dropped books.

"Why isn't it my turn, miss, I've worked ever so hard?" pleaded Sam.

"It is not for us to question the headmaster's judgment," said Susan, although she felt that a big mistake had been made. Well, Mr. Corrie would soon find out and it would serve him right. It would be very difficult to instil the virtues of hard work into her class if the headmaster was going to be so arbitrary in his choice of pupil.

"It isn't fair!" wailed Sam.

"Nobody above the age of nine expects life to be fair," she said. Susan was now on firmer ground, but she felt sorry for Sam. "You are now the best pupil in the class, and I will promote you to pen and ink which means that you can be ink monitor." She tried not to think about the mess; it would give the children some ambition, and she could appoint a 'mopping up' monitor later.

Watching Sam start to smile, and the other children admiring his pen, Susan felt that the natural order had been restored. Mr. Corrie would soon realize his mistake; in the meantime, he and Tommy deserved each other. She asked the next child to resume reading, and suddenly a dark cloud lifted from her class. God had taken the offending child off her hands for a while, and that was fine as long as nobody thought that she couldn't manage to deal with a naughty boy. With a bit of luck, Mr. Corrie might not admit that he had been wrong. She looked at her class and realized that it would be easier to manage.

"Stop snivelling, Deborah, your brother is next door, not on the other side of the world."

16 THE GODFATHER

Ben breathed a sigh of relief when he reached the next classroom, and realized that nobody was going to send him back. He felt that everyone was looking at him as the two newcomers stood in front of the class, waiting to be told which desk to use. Mr. Corrie directed some of the boys to move desks; his best scholars received the prized desks at the back and the younger children and troublemakers were nearer to the teacher's desk. The two newcomers shared a double desk at the front right hand corner of the room, but were told that they would be moved if their work was good.

Mr. Corrie explained what was expected of them. Ben's attention had only just started to wander when a small piece of chalk hit him on the ear and everybody laughed. He later found out that Mr. Corrie could throw chalk very accurately with either hand and sometimes the children laid bets on who would be the next target.

The reading lesson was very different from that in the previous class. Ben was given a piece to read in his own time, and then answer questions on his slate. He looked around; two of the older girls were listening to younger children reading aloud, but he and Jack were expected to read silently and answer questions. He was enjoying the feeling of being grown up, sitting and looking around while Jack was writing away next to him. Mr. Corrie picked up another piece of chalk and looked at Ben, who started writing his answers to the questions. Some children had finished their work and taken it to be marked; those without corrections were permitted to choose a school library book from the back of the class, which seemed an exciting idea to Ben, who started making a bit more effort. Unfortunately, by the time he had finished the work and his corrections, the lesson was over and it was time for arithmetic.

***

After a few days Ben gained the privilege of choosing a book, and lessons seemed much better than they had been in his Aunt Susan's class. He had thought that if he were in Mr. Corrie's class, then school would be wonderful, with nothing to complain about. The lessons were fine, he was learning to dodge the chalk, but he didn't like sharing a double desk with Jack Harrison. Jack was a tall awkward looking lad, his hair looked as if he had been through a hedge backwards, and he had taken a dislike to Ben. Maybe it was because Ben had taken a place that rightly belonged to Jack's best friend Sam, maybe because he just didn't like him. Ben kept calling Jack 'Johnny' because of his resemblance to Johnny Harrison; that did not help, and they were glad to get away from each other by the end of the first week.

On the next Monday, they divided their desk down the middle, using a pencil mark that was already there, and they threatened to fight each other if any possessions or elbows were found on the wrong side of the line. Relations worsened as the week went on; there seemed to be fewer and fewer children in class, and there was talk of measles. Ben wondered what measles were, and could he have some – he would quite like to stay and play at the forge during the day as long as Aunt Susan remained in front of her class.

There did not seem to be many children playing tag at playtime, and he and Jack spent their time shouting insults at each other.

"Lofty!"

"Titch!"

"Scarecrow!"

"Sweep!"

By Friday Ben was feeling quite cross and tired, and deliberately let his elbow stray on to the wrong side of the desk, just to see what would happen. The fight was arranged for playtime and he looked forward to it as he had run out of insults.

When the time came, the older children were impressed that both boys were in the playground ready to fight, and were not cowering in the privies, needing to be dragged out. The older children formed a ring around the boys, who were very evenly matched. Jack was taller, with a longer reach, but missed his target some of the time. Ben was quite fast on his feet, but felt unusually clumsy and tired and neither of the boys was punching as hard as they usually would. They kept up the insults and the crowd cheered them on.

"You're like a little black beetle!"

"Your hair is like a raggy mat!"

"You don't even belong here!"

SELINA STANGER

"What's the weather like up in the clouds?"

"Crawl back under your stone!"

Out of the corner of his eye, Ben could see his Aunt Susan. Jack's sister was pointing the fight out to her, just in case she was in any doubt. I'm in trouble now, thought Ben, but Mr. Corrie got to the boys first.

"Break it up lads, wait for me in my study. The rest of you, back to class since you don't seem to want to play," said Mr. Corrie.

The other children went reluctantly back to class, turning occasionally to see what Ben and Jack were going to do. The lads felt that honour was more or less satisfied; they felt tired but could not resist one final insult.

"You are ugly and spotty!"

"Not as spotty as you!"

"You are both very spotty; it is probably measles," said Mr. Corrie, and sent one of the children to fetch Dr. Harrison.

Jack and Ben sank gratefully on to a small bench in Mr. Corrie's study; a small anteroom next to his classroom that also served as a storeroom. They looked around in wonder; neither of them had seen so many books before. They waited in silence, wondering how many strokes of the cane they would get and which of Mr. Corrie's hands would deliver the sentence. But the cane stayed on its hook on the wall. Ben's head ached and the light hurt his eyes; he thought that if this was measles he should be more careful what he wished for.

A large man arrived, filling the doorframe as he walked in. Ben thought he had seen him before, the night he arrived, but wasn't sure. The man's face and hair resembled Jack's and Johnny's so Ben thought that the measles must have been making his wits addled.

"Thank you for coming so promptly, doctor, I think that both these lads might have measles," said Mr. Corrie.

"They look as if they have been fighting," said the man.

"Sorry, Uncle Tom," said Jack. If this was Jack's uncle, Ben thought he might be in even more trouble.

"Sorry, sir," said Ben.

"Don't you know who I am?" asked the doctor.

"No sir, sorry, sir," said Ben.

"I am Dr. Tom Harrison, Jack's uncle, Johnny Harrison's uncle and your godfather. So you two are family and should be friends. I spend half of my life patching people up after fights as it is!" said the doctor.

"But he said…" but Ben could not remember what Jack had said to him, and it did not seem to matter anymore.

"You two boys must go home and not come back here until Dr. Harrison says that you are better," said Mr. Corrie, "there will be no punishment unless I catch you fighting again."

Ben's eyes filled with tears as he remembered his real home, and he failed to notice his Aunt Susan coming into the room.

"I don't suppose you could keep your godson at your house for a while, Dr. Harrison," she said, "my sister has enough to do, looking after poor Dickon, without running around after this one."

"Aunt Sally is ever so sick, every morning," said Ben, "but I would be no trouble, honest."

"Ben can stay with me for a while; our charwoman can keep an eye on him during the day when we are out," said the doctor. "Come along Jack, your house is on the way."

***

Ben did not remember much of the next two weeks, except for lying in a darkened room and having his eyes bathed every morning before they would open. Then one morning he could sit up in bed without feeling dizzy; he was in the room where he and his brother had spent their first night away from their village. The room looked just the same with its large double bed and several interesting looking chests and cupboards, and he amused himself by counting the cobwebs on the ceiling and walls.

He felt really hungry but when he was given a slice of bread and jam, he could only finish half of it. He looked forward to the next day when he was allowed to get up, but felt very wobbly and weak, and had to sit down on one of the chests, which creaked alarmingly. Gradually he regained his strength, and there was talk of him going back to school the next Monday. Ben started exploring the house, with its odd rooms, cupboards, strange objects and books and realized that he felt really at home in the chaos. Perhaps there was a way he could stay there a bit longer, and not go back to his Aunt Susan just yet.

***

On Friday morning, Ben was well enough to go outside, and he spent a happy morning playing with Jack, making boats and sailing them in the stream. Their differences seemed to be forgotten, as the other children were at school and the forge was out of bounds.

After dinner there was no sign of Jack, so Ben stayed in the shop with Charlie, dusting shelves and listening to tales of Charlie's first days at the surgery as a twelve-year-old apprentice. Suddenly a panic-stricken Jack came rushing in, asking if Dr. Harrison could come and see his baby sister right away as she was very poorly. As Dr. Harrison was dealing with a difficult confinement some miles away, Charlie gathered his bag, prepared to set off, and then hesitated.

"Ben, please mind the shop for a little while; it is a pity to lose sales and I probably will be back soon," said Charlie.

"How do I do that? I don't know what everything is or how much it costs! I might sell the wrong thing and poison someone," said Ben.

"Just remember what people want, and you can deliver it later, just like I used to do. There is a slate and some chalk somewhere, just try your best and guess at the spelling; we'll work out what they want later," said Charlie before he was almost dragged out of the shop by a very impatient Jack.

Ben felt very important as he stood in the shop pretending that it was his, but hoping that the customers wouldn't want anything difficult. Half an hour passed, and nobody came in. Ben sat down behind the counter but got up in a hurry when he heard the bell ring. His first customer was Arthur Brown from the ale house. Ben proudly wrote his name and the word 'TONNIK' on his slate. By the end of the afternoon, he had quite a long list and his writing was getting quite small and squashed; he hoped he would be able to remember everything when Charlie came back. The door opened quietly without the bell. Ben was bent over his slate and did not notice his Aunt Susan come in.

"I see you are better; you were seen out playing this morning. You must come back to the forge with me now, and return to school on Monday," said Susan.

"The doctors are both out, and I'm minding the shop for Dr. Charlie. I need to stay for a while until he comes back," said Ben. He hid his slate behind his back, because of the spellings he wasn't sure of.

"I don't see how you can be doing anything useful, so just get your things and come with me. I am very surprised that you have been trusted to look after the shop. I will have a word with Dr. Charlie, later," said Susan.

"I have a whole long list of orders, which will be delivered when one of the doctors comes back to mix the medicines up and put them in bottles. Dr. Harrison is at one of the farms some miles away and Dr. Charlie was called out very suddenly to Jack Harrison's baby sister. Dr. Charlie will probably be back soon, but he told me to mind the shop and I haven't any keys to lock up," said Ben.

"Well, I'm glad you can make yourself useful, it makes a change," said Susan, "but if you're not back by mid-morning tomorrow, I will come and fetch you."

Ben decided that he would offer to help the doctors with the medicine deliveries the next day, so that he would be out next time his aunt called.

17 THE MEASLES

Charlie was worried about the baby he had visited the previous day; she had seemed to be recovering but then went down with another fever. He was glad that Tom had offered to go and visit; it was his brother's family after all, and Charlie thought that the baby deserved a more experienced doctor. He worked away, mixing medicines and cutting pills, and was surprised and pleased when Ben offered to deliver the orders to the customers.

Charlie was concerned about the work that had to be done; the measles epidemic meant that both doctors were called out a lot more, and it was a godsend having a young boy available to run errands. In the absence of the charwoman, Charlie usually made the dinner on Saturdays, but a makeshift meal of bread and cheese was looking more and more likely. Charlie was absolutely delighted when Ben arrived, staggering under the weight of three large meat and potato pies.

"I thought you wouldn't have time to make dinner, and I don't know how, so I bought these," said Ben. "Here is the money from the customers, less the cost of the pies; they look really good don't they?"

Charlie quickly pushed aside the medicine bottles to make space on the table for two of the pies; the third was put on the top of the stove to keep warm for Tom. They quickly made a start on their dinner, and did not bother to look for knives and forks.

When Susan arrived to fetch her nephew home for dinner at the forge, she was not best pleased to find him very much at home at the surgery. She noticed the untidy kitchen, pills all over the floor and shuddered at the dinner table with its medicines, papers and goodness knows what else.

"Charlie! This lad was supposed to be back at the forge by now; his dinner is waiting. It is very kind of you to look after him, but I have come to relieve you of your responsibilities," said Susan.

Charlie was not aware that Ben was expected back, and was about to say so when he noticed an imploring look from Ben, who gazed up at him hopefully with his mouth full of pie and gravy all down his chin.

"I am ever so sorry; we've been so busy we haven't had time to think. It would be really good if you could spare Ben for a little longer," he said. "If he delivers the parcels, I can keep the shop open this afternoon."

"I suppose so, if you really think he can be useful. I doubt it, myself."

"It would be good if he could help out for a while and the crisis should be over soon."

"You spoil that child.! Don't let him get his feet under the table, I expect him back at school on Monday."

Ben looked at his feet; they were under the table, but where else would they be? Once his aunt had gone, he cut an uneven doorstep of bread and used it to mop up the gravy that had spilt on the table and was heading towards a pile of papers.

"Don't you want to go back yet? Don't you miss your brother?"

"Dickon is always in the forge with Uncle Kit, and I always seem to be in the way in the kitchen. I really like staying here. If I promise to go back to school on Monday, do you think you might have a few odd jobs for me to do afterwards?"

"You will have to ask your godfather," said Charlie, "but I see no reason why not."

***

Tom came back wearily that evening after the death of his baby niece, and did not even notice that Ben was still there. Charlie tried to make Tom eat something, but he had no appetite for the pie and they knew there would be no time to cook anything else before they were called out again.

The few days that followed seemed very dark. Tom was weighed down by sorrow, but it was not only the funeral of his brother's child that brought him down. As a professional man he hated to watch the town's children succumb one by one to measles, and he knew that many of them would be too weak to fight the other illnesses that would follow. Tom had brought many of the children into the world and could only stand by helplessly as a large number of them were maimed or worse.

Charlie held things together as best he could, but he could see why being a doctor was so difficult at times like these. Tom was quiet and withdrawn; he seemed to have grown old in the last few weeks, and Charlie did not think he could have been more than about thirty. Charlie did not mention the fact that no word had come about Benjie's funeral; he supposed the letter must have been lost as the mail coach travelled across the wild moors. Charlie also had expected Nancy's effects would have been sent to Tom by now, but he had not said anything and Charlie did not like to raise the subject.

***

On the Friday evening, Charlie struggled with the accounts, his head aching after a late night on call the night before. The books were open on the table, together with the remains of a makeshift meal and some partially completed orders for medicines. He was not pleased to hear a knock at the door.

"Look at the state of you," said Susan kindly, "couldn't anyone clear up so that you could use the table?"

"Ben wanted to do it, "said Charlie, "but I sent him to bed because he has worked hard every evening after school, and only just recovered from the measles himself."

"It's been a terrible week, there so many children away and the playground is very quiet. The worst thing is knowing that some of my class won't be coming back to school."

"Some children died, some were left blind or deaf, and some lost their wits. I feel sorry for that poor blind girl and her grandmother who have to go the workhouse."

"Last time I heard they were knitting for some of the draper's shops, so they might manage to keep themselves with their work."

"That's good news, but our patients won't all be so lucky. I don't know how we would have managed without Ben this week, he has been doing a lot of the jobs an apprentice would do – it frees us up to visit patients and make up medicines."

"Let me do the adding up for you. I am sure you have more important things to do," said Susan as Charlie gratefully pushed the books towards her through the breadcrumbs. "Are the entries up to date?"

"No, here are today's orders. Ben has delivered some of them, and marked the ones that are paid," said Charlie, passing her Ben's slate.

Susan looked at the slate; the writing was clear enough, but the spelling was interesting with several orders for 'lordnum' and 'baccy'.

"It looks as if he can read and write," she said. "He showed no sign of it when he was in my class. Hopefully his spelling will improve."

"Tom said that Ben would make a good apprentice when he is older," said Charlie. "We could keep the practice in the family."

Susan sat back as if a great weight had been taken off her shoulders.

"Does Tom really think so? I was so worried that Ben 'as you call him' would not be able to earn a living. He's no scholar, and he never seemed to remember what he had been asked to do, and I thought he would end up in the workhouse or worse. It may look as if I am hard on him, but I am doing it for his own good."

"Ben is very clever, like Nancy, but he gets bored easily and then his mind can go wandering off on its own. He doesn't always hear what is said when he is daydreaming. Adam Corrie says that he is getting better but he still has to throw chalk at him occasionally! Both Tom and I would be more than happy to employ Ben when the time comes."

"That is a real weight off my mind. I thought he had been damaged by what he saw when…" She trailed off and then said, "and maybe his wits were addled."

"I don't think that Ben saw very much," said Charlie, "but his imagination will fill in the gaps, poor lad. However, plenty of children have seen worse, and they just have to get on with things as best they can. I know you were worried about how Ben would manage if we weren't here to look after him, but he will make his way in the world just fine."

"And you really find him useful here?"

"Very much, especially at the moment; it's handy to have someone to run a few errands, and mind the shop in an emergency. Charlie did not say that Ben had adopted one of the attic rooms and had been slowly gathering his things and settling in.

"In that case, if he's not in the way, I don't mind if he stays a bit longer and helps you out after school. I would like him to come to us for Sunday dinner, before he forgets how to use a knife and fork properly. It mightn't do you and Dr. Tom any harm either."

"You are just what I need, to make me fit company for you fine ladies at the forge," said Charlie, tugging his forelock.

"I will have a bit more time to oversee the repairs to the cottages, if I am not chasing after young Ben all the time."

"It's been very difficult recently but in a few months we will be married and everything will be wonderful. What could possibly go wrong?"

The work on the medicines and the books slowed down a little as the young couple concentrated more on each other, and their future together.

18 THE GIFT

Charlie woke up on a beautiful April morning without a care in the world. He was a qualified surgeon and a partner in the practice so he could earn his living and support a family. Better still, Susan had agreed to marry him; they had listened to their banns being read out in church for the third time the day before. He opened his window, and as he appreciated the fresh clean air and the birdsong, he became aware that there were more people than usual in the street below.

Susan was going to marry him, although for some reason she wanted to live in one of her cottages rather than at the surgery, but Charlie was content as it would be quite near to where he worked. He would have enjoyed this moment for a bit longer, but there seemed to be a queue of customers waiting for him to open the shop.

"I looked out of my window, and someone has left a basket on the doorstep," shouted Ben as he clattered down from his attic.

"Did it look like something nice? A twenty first birthday present from a grateful patient?" asked Charlie, getting out the keys so that they could open the shop.

"It looked more like a bundle of washing," answered Ben, "you can just see it from this angle."

Charlie saw the basket, and the bundle of washing seemed to move. He put the keys back in his pocket as he saw two small fists waving from the basket. It was quite normal for a desperate mother to leave a baby at the workhouse, but unusual for her to leave it at the surgery.

"Let's just go downstairs and bring it in; don't say anything to the crowd or answer their questions," said Charlie, "it's too early to open the shop just yet."

They were very quiet as they brought in the surprise gift, but the basket contents made enough noise for the three of them. Sweeping aside the clutter on the kitchen table, Charlie put down the basket, and looked into a small face with a shock of black hair and eyes as blue as his own.

"Be sure your sins will find you out." Tom was trying to keep his face straight. "When Ben has gone to school, you and I will have a little talk."

***

"A healthy baby girl, about three months old," said Tom, "and she looks very much like you. There's no note in the basket; have you any idea who the mother might be?"

"I am not sure," said Charlie, "when I was a journeyman, two of my landladies challenged my virtue; they were looking for comfort on cold dark nights and what's a man to do? And there might have been other occasions when a lady forced her attentions on me. But I thought I was careful."

"You must have some idea who the mother might be." The baby was scowling, yelling and waving her fists. "It's obvious who the father is."

"She does look like me, doesn't she? Look at that beak of a nose, it's all wrong on a girl, she must have a strong character," said Charlie proudly as he poured a little milk into a bowl and cut a slice of bread.

"She'll need to have, with those looks," said Tom, watching her sucking milk from the bread. "That's better, nice and quiet. Could the mother be one of your landladies?"

"Could be either of them, I wouldn't like to question the honour of either of those good ladies. They would deny it anyway, as the baby could be inconvenient if a husband came home after a long absence," said Charlie, enjoying the silence as the baby fed.

"So what will you do if the baby cannot be taken back to her mother?" asked Tom. "Will you take her to the workhouse?"

Charlie was trying to concentrate on feeding the baby, who had finished the milk and was starting on the bread. She impatiently bit his finger; he jumped and she giggled. Tom quickly poured more milk into the bowl.

"Small babies don't usually thrive in the workhouse without their mothers. They are fed and kept clean but somehow it isn't enough." Charlie looked at the baby, who was smiling at him. "I could call her Maria after my mother, she had a lovely sweet gentle nature."

"She looks, and sounds, more like your late unlamented grandmother, Martha," said Tom, "but you can't keep her here. Looking after a baby is a full time job, and you can't let her distract us from our work."

"Do you think you could find a nurse nearby, until she is a bit older?" He did not mention Susan; he was trying not to think about what she would say.

"I'll see what I can do, but it'll cost you," said Tom. "Jeannie might be glad of some extra money, now George is on short time at the mill." He did not mention Susan either.

"I'll have to tell Susan, but I don't want to disturb her at the school," said Charlie. Perhaps if he registered the birth first, so that there was no going back, he could persuade Susan later.

***

Queuing at the registry door and carrying the basket, Charlie was not so sure that it was a good idea. All the townspeople seemed very interested in what he was carrying; they were crowding round and making comments.

"What a funny little baby!"

"He'll grow into that face!"

"The baby is a girl," said Charlie.

"Oh dear, what a shame."

"You know who she reminds me of?"

"With that black hair and beak of a nose, she looks just like Martha Armstrong!"

Some people crossed themselves, and others crossed the street but still more came to look. The registrar came out to see what the fuss was about. It was a very trying morning; many people had deaths to register. One of his assistants had a very delicate stomach, and was having trouble recording the cause of death as the customers were deliberately giving much more detail than was needed.

And there was Charlie, who seemed to be getting a lot of attention and disturbing the smooth running of the office even more.

"Well, we are keeping a lot of you good people from your work, so we will have to speed things up a bit. You, lad," he said turning to the assistant who was looking a little green, "might find it a little easier to register the births. Very straightforward, mother's name, father's name if possible, date and place of birth, name of baby. Queue this side for births, and my other lad will write down the details of the deaths."

The onlookers grumbled a little as they were deprived of their fun, but were distracted by Charlie's basket as he waited to register the birth.

"Ooh look, she's waking up and waving her little fists."

"Just like Martha, look at that scowl, isn't that the beginnings of a squint?"

"No it isn't," said Charlie, "lots of babies do that. The baby was beginning to complain a little, and he wished he were back in the surgery.

"Mother's name?" asked the assistant.

"I'm not sure," said Charlie. "Does it matter?" The baby was getting louder.

"What do I do?" shouted the assistant. "We have to have the mother's name."

"Just leave it blank for now," said the registrar, raising his voice.

"Father's name?" asked the assistant.

"That's easy," answered someone in the crowd, "just look at her!"

The paternity was unmistakable, and Charlie slowly spelt out his name for the lad filling in the form.

"Name of the baby?"

Charlie was saying 'Maria', but everyone else had put 'Martha' into his mind. Charlie closed his ears to the crowd and helpfully spelled out 'Maria', a pretty gentle name, something for his daughter to live up to. He imagined a pretty, dainty, fragrant girl, but it was difficult with her features and he caught a whiff of a very different fragrance from the depths of the basket.

"When was she born?" asked the lad, who was struggling a bit with the fragrance.

"I think she's about three or four months old," said Charlie, helpfully.

The baby was moving about quite a lot by now; the lad was estimating a date of birth and was counting on his fingers, but found it difficult to concentrate. Finally, he gave in, and rushed out of the room with his hand over his mouth.

"How difficult can it be to register a birth?" asked the registrar. "Oh, I see, just put the basket in that corner near the door for a little while. I am sure the baby needs some fresh air."

Charlie gratefully followed the suggestion, hoping that the crowd would follow the baby and give him some privacy, but nobody wanted to miss any of the conversation.

"You have been a naughty boy, Charlie," said the registrar, "where was the baby born?"

Charlie was reminded of the days when he was a young boy in the poorhouse, called into the master's office to account for some misdemeanour. He found himself hanging his head and shuffling his feet.

"I'm not sure where she was born, either," said Charlie.

"You must know who the mother is. Presumably she isn't a local girl?" asked the registrar.

"That's just it, I'm not sure who it could be," said Charlie.

"Are you saying that several ladies had their wicked way with you a year ago?" asked the registrar. "You've been a very naughty boy."

"That is the case and I would not want to besmirch an innocent lady's reputation," said Charlie. He held his head up this time as the registrar was smiling at him and the crowd was impressed, he could tell.

"Who would have thought it?"

"Charlie's been putting himself about a bit!"

"Didn't know he had it in him!"

"And shall I arrange for the baby to go straight to the workhouse, since her mother has obviously abandoned her?" asked the registrar.

"No, I shall bring her up as best I can," said Charlie. He hoped that Tom had been successful in finding a nurse as the baby had needs that Charlie would find difficult to meet on a regular basis.

"Very impressive, a man who can shoulder his responsibilities," said the registrar as he wrote out the certificate and handed it to Charlie.

"I named the baby Maria, but the certificate says 'Martha'," said Charlie.

"Not a problem, we will give her the middle name 'Maria'," said the registrar. "If you christen her 'Maria' and always call her 'Maria' you will have no problem."

Charlie left with the praises of the crowd ringing in his ears.

"Bringing up young Martha himself!"

"Shouldering his burden like a man!".

"Good old Charlie Sawbones!"

"Such an ill-favoured child as well."

"He will have trouble getting her off his hands, especially with that squint!"

"Even more if she turns out like her namesake!"

She doesn't have a squint, thought Charlie, her eyes are fine; it is her nose that could be a problem.

Charlie walked home with his head held high, trying not to think of the person who would definitely not be impressed.

***

"Jeannie said she would look after the baby for us, at the normal rate, but I think that you should change and feed the baby first, just in case she changes her mind," said Tom

"I'll make sure that my daughter is 'nice to know' before I take her to Jeannie," said Charlie.

He looked to see if there was space on the table to change the baby, but the table was covered in its usual clutter; in fact an extra layer had been deposited during the course of the day. In the end Charlie decided to leave the baby in the basket; it took him a while before she was clean and wrapped in a sheet, the rest of her possessions rinsed out and in a little damp bundle. And the baby did not agree with Charlie's priorities as she felt that she had a more pressing need for bread and milk. In the confusion neither of the men noticed a small envelope fall behind the mattress, and the baby did not care.

Later, both men were grateful for the silence, punctuated by sucking and slurping noises. After the bread and milk was finished, the baby wailed reproachfully and a second helping was hastily provided before she slept contentedly.

"I am surprised she ate all that, she must be full by now."

"Absolutely podged!" answered Charlie with a smile, carefully wiping a small dribble of milk from the baby's mouth.

"Let's get young Martha to Jeannie's before she wakes up." Tom was looking at the certificate.

"I called her Maria, but the people were making so much noise that the clerk wrote 'Martha' instead of 'Maria'. She will be known by her middle name."

But the moment had passed and the baby was always known as Martha, and Charlie forgot to rectify the matter at her christening.

19 THE CHURCH

Susan sat in her classroom, grateful for a short rest while the children played in the playground after their dinner. It had been a very difficult few months for everyone, with the measles epidemic taking a heavy toll. Susan had struggled even more than most, coming to terms with the breakup of her family after her father's death and the arrival of her nephews. She did not want to think about what had happened to her sister Nancy, and had successfully blanked it from her mind, at least most of the time. At three o'clock in the morning she usually found herself trying to think of more possibilities but there only seemed to be the one grim scenario.

Susan felt she was turning a corner, and the little house would be ready to move into after her wedding in a few days' time. Charlie loved her and would always be there for her, and life would become safe and predictable again. Susan hoped that the wedding would go smoothly, with her sister Sally as matron of honour. All the girls in her class had wanted to be bridesmaids, and she had put her foot down firmly and refused to consider fifteen bridesmaids with varying shapes, sizes and competence. She compromised and said that they could form a guard of honour holding garlands on the church steps. That way they would be firmly outside the church, and not milling about inside; as long as the garlands were not used as weapons everything would be all right.

Susan heard more noise than usual, so she had a look out into the yard. The children were very excitable, running about and giggling and occasionally glancing at her window. Adam and Elizabeth came out of the schoolhouse, and she overheard them discussing some problem or other.

"I think it would be more suitable if you told her."

"I don't know what to say, I was so shocked."

"The news would be better, coming from you."

"What about the children?"

"They can play out for a bit longer, it won't hurt them."

Susan wondered whom they were talking about, and was very surprised when Elizabeth came into her classroom and said that they needed to have a little talk.

***

"So that's all I know. I thought that it was better that I told you than if you heard it from the children," said Elizabeth. "I must say that I'm not surprised."

"Where's the baby now?" asked Susan, hoping that Charlie was not expecting her to look after his by-blow.

"I heard that Dr. Harrison was looking for a local woman to nurse her, as the doctors needed to get on with their work. Tending children always falls to women."

Susan was grateful that she was not expected to drop everything and mind some other woman's baby, but felt that she should at least have been consulted. The world expected her to speed off to see the baby and take her in her arms, amid a rush of maternal feeling, but she felt angry. Susan felt that she could not bring herself to ask after the baby, and whether she was thriving, but Elizabeth answered that one for her.

"Young Martha is a healthy baby, but a bit odd looking. She looks very much like her namesake, apparently."

Susan remembered Charlie's ill-natured grandmother and shuddered. The old lady had tried to kidnap Charlie to join the gang of labourers that she ruled with a rod of iron. Following the tragic events after Benjie and Nancy's elopement, old Martha accused them of stealing her horse and nearly got them hung.

"I can't say that it's a surprise; your Charlie was brought up in the poorhouse and learnt nasty low ways but my Adam would behave with more propriety. But who are we to criticize the ways of men? We just have to put up with whatever they do."

Susan felt like saying that was not the way things worked in her house, and that Charlie would expect (and get) a modicum of criticism. But Elizabeth and Adam were her employers until the new teacher arrived in September, so she had to tread carefully. Adam and Elizabeth had been married a few years and there was no sign of a baby, which was a pity as Elizabeth actually liked children. Susan thought that there was only one thing worse than children, and that was people. She thanked Elizabeth for taking the trouble to talk to her, and went to her classroom as the children filed in.

"There's ever such an ugly baby come to live at our house," said Deborah Harrison, and the children all looked at one another and giggled.

***

Susan and Charlie were on their own at the surgery; Tom had gone out on his rounds and discreetly taken Ben with him. The kitchen had been swept and looked much tidier than usual and Charlie stood in front of Susan with his head bowed and his hat in his hands.

"I don't know how it could have happened!"

Susan knew exactly how these things happened, and said so.

"You made love to someone else when you were promised to me! There is no excuse."

"I am truly sorry, Susan, please forgive me." He looked an abject figure as he stood looking at his feet.

"How do I know it wouldn't happen again if we were married?"

"It will never happen again, with you beside me I would never even look at another woman. Us men are very weak but the love of a good woman keeps us on the right track." He looked up, and gave her his best smile.

"And you behaved irresponsibly."

"I know and I'm sorry, but I'm accepting my responsibilities now and will do right by my daughter."

"And you expect me to raise her?"

"It would be unfair of me to ask you. Maria can stay with Jeannie until she starts school, even longer if you prefer. I will visit her discreetly." A change came over his face when he thought about his baby, smiling and giggling or yelling and waving her fists; he was equally smitten either way.

"I hear she's not a prepossessing baby."

"She has an interesting face," answered Charlie, "and she will have a difficult time making her way in the world."

It was mainly Charlie's attitude to the baby that changed Susan's mind, after all most men would shake a loose leg if they were given half the chance. But not many would be prepared to do right by a baby who had been abandoned with nobody to fight her corner.

"Let's go and see your daughter," said Susan, standing up and putting her hand on Charlie's shoulder.

***

Susan felt very conspicuous as she walked to the church with Kit and Sally on her wedding day. Her veil was blowing all over the place, her bouquet was scratchy and awkward; she was sure that people were whispering about her but tried not to listen.

"A real charmer, that one! He could easily talk her round!"

"Saddling her with his baby!"

"I thought Jeannie was looking after young Martha."

"After the wedding she will have to do as he tells her."

"She won't like that very much!"

"More fool her for marrying him."

Susan was beginning to doubt her first generous reaction to Charlie's misdemeanour. For one thing she hadn't seen much of Charlie, he was either working or visiting the baby. She was wondering if she was doing the right thing marrying Charlie, or if he would always have a tendency to stray. He was always kind to other people, but would she take second place to anyone with a sob story? And now she was hearing how things appeared to other people, and it hurt her pride.

"The Grahams used to hold their heads up in the town, but now they are just like the rest of us."

"It all started when Nancy ran off with Benjie Armstrong."

"Sally married someone from the poorhouse, his family weren't up to much."

"Richard Graham spoilt those girls!"

"And now Susan's marrying a man who can't be trusted."

"He could charm the ducks off the pond. I wouldn't mind a roll in the hay with him."

"I don't think I'd marry him though, he's trouble, just like his cousin Benjie."

"I heard that…"

Susan gritted her teeth and walked on grimly, glad the veil was hiding her face. She would not let the whispers worry her, she was nearly at the church where everyone would be silent; she only had to get past the ramshackle guard of honour at the door.

"Get that garland from up my nose or I will bat you with it!"

"It isn't me, it's Deborah."

"Get off my foot or I will tell miss."

"Miss is busy, marrying that bad lad."

"I think she's silly."

My mother said he's no better than he should be."

"She'll be sorry."

Susan ignored them as she walked through the door, trying to hold her head up, but feeling more and more angry. There were all her friends and neighbours looking at her, and then looking at each other. She saw Charlie at the front, sharing a joke with Tom; his shoulders always shook when he laughed. What was he laughing at? Was it the fact that he had charmed his way back into her good graces after doing something unforgivable? Well she wasn't going to forgive him!

The bouquet was dropping bits as Susan walked down the aisle; her veil was in the way as she tried to keep it all together and was getting more and more angry. Charlie was still laughing; he hadn't even turned around. How dare he make her a laughing stock! She held the bouquet high in her right hand, aimed and hurled it at Charlie as only a blacksmith's daughter could. The veil fell off; she stamped on it, and jumped up and down for good measure.

Susan stalked out of the church with her head held high and did not look back. She heard a gasp (probably Elizabeth) followed by a silence and just kept walking. She heard someone say 'Good for her!' and there was a faint cheer from some of the women. Smiling to herself, she kept walking.

20 – 1842 - THE RIOTS

Time had moved on after the dramatic events of 1839 and Charlie's three-year-old daughter Martha was still being fostered by Tom's brother George and sister-in-law Jeannie. Susan and Charlie were never completely reconciled and remained unmarried. Dickon was helping Kit in the forge. Sally taught him his letters as best she could but the blacksmith's accounts and her own growing family kept her busy.

Ben was settled at the doctor's house (ensconced according to Tom) and he took care to make himself useful so that there was no question of him living at the forge. He visited his brother Dickon, and Tom thought he was avoiding his Aunt Susan for some reason, but it was very difficult to understand what was going on in Ben's head.

Tom and his brothers were in the ale house following the funeral of their father, John, who had passed away after a long battle with consumption. Tom's brother George lived locally and his eldest brother Joe had travelled from Hilltop where he was working as a brewer. Tom's youngest brother Robert had settled in the North East, working as a platelayer on the new railway, and had picked up the hard drinking, plain speaking culture as well as the Darlington accent. Tom's brother-in-law headmaster Adam (married to sister Elizabeth) and brother-in-law newspaperman Henry (married to sister Mary Ann) had made their excuses and left the wake as soon as was polite.

Tom tried to make himself heard above the noise of the ale house. He and his brothers had sung at the church, sorrowed at the graveside and bonded over tea with the womenfolk. It now was time for serious drinking - as was usual on such occasions - and Tom was trying to attract Arthur's attention to bespeak the wheelbarrow for Robert at the end of the evening.

"I can hold my drink fine now, man!" protested Robert. "Save the wheelbarrow for those that can't. It wasn't just me that time at George's wedding."

"We've just buried our dad," soothed Joe, "we shouldn't be arguing."

But everyone was looking at George who had struggled to his feet to say that he could hold his drink as well as any man, he just felt a bit tired right now. He was still protesting when they picked him up off the floor.

"Look at him, man, there's nothing of him, he's as light as a feather to pick up," said Robert. "Tom, I thought you were supposed to be looking after the family!"

"Stop fussing, I'm fine," retorted George, "Talking of family, where's Adam?"

"He stayed with the womenfolk, I think he's reading poetry to them. Charlie says he's becoming quite an old woman himself, and is no good as a drinking partner any more. All this school mastering is addling his brain. I always thought it wasn't a real man's job," said Tom.

"Have you been to the doctors to see what's wrong?" Robert asked George, ignoring Tom.

"Where did young Henry get to?" asked George, "I thought he would have stayed longer."

"He went back to Carlisle with Mary Ann," answered Tom, "They were both very anxious to get back, you know what newlyweds are like!"

"On that lonely road, in the dark, at this time of night?" asked Joe.

"They travelled on the new railway," answered Tom, "rather them than me."

"I told you the railways were coming," boasted Robert. "All that hard work and invention, we'll be able to go all over the country soon. And I'm helping to build the track; they couldn't do it without the track."

"It'll be a long time before the railways get to us at Hilltop," said Joe. "We're really out in the sticks."

"Don't be too sure, they're looking for a way to carry the mail from London," said Robert," then the mail coach won't stop here anymore and Arthur will be out of a job. Hey, Arthur, this jug is empty!"

"We'll always keep Arthur busy," answered Tom, as he ordered another jug.

"Haven't you lot got homes to go to?" grumbled Arthur as he brought the ale.

Robert noticed George's hand shaking as he picked up his tankard.

"You don't look well at all, George," said Robert in a worried voice, "and we've only just buried dad."

"George and I both know what's wrong," explained Tom. "He's consumptive; most mill workers get it eventually. I've been trying to persuade him to have treatment, perhaps you can do better."

"It doesn't always kill," retorted George "it might shorten the life down to forty or so but most people are finished by then, especially mill workers."

"Come and stay with me," suggested Joe. "Our bracing fresh air will make the difference and you would be better in no time."

"I've a family to look after," argued George, who would not admit that he was struggling with short time work.

"You could at least have treatment from the doctors," said Robert. "They treat their own families for free."

"I'll take no man's charity!" said George.

"Charlie has offered him our best laudanum, and first choice of the leeches from the jar, but it makes no difference," said Tom. He tried not to think of Charlie's family; cousin Benjie would never need their services anymore.

"Come and stay with me, then," invited Joe. "I could use the company, and you can bring your family as well."

"I would rather stay here, then if anything happens Jeannie is among our own people," answered George,

"You have a point," said Joe, thoughtfully. "I thought Benjie and Nancy were well settled but the squire took against them."

"What exactly did happen?" asked Tom, plying Joe with drink.

"Well," said Joe, and took a long draught, "Milady…"

There was a loud crash as a paving stone flew into the room, followed by most of the window, and they realized the cause of the noise outside. The cold wind blew in rain and dust from the street and the peace of the ale house was shattered. Nobody ventured to look out, for fear of other missiles but they heard shouts and screams, and were in no doubt that a full-scale riot was going on.

***

They all helped to board up the offending window, and all the other windows for good measure. Arthur locked and barred all the doors, while the brothers cleared the broken glass, then he fetched another jug and advised that they should all stay inside until things settled down.

"I thought I lived in a hard place where men lose their tempers easily, but I've seen nothing like this!" exclaimed Robert.

"Young Charlie's going to be busy tonight," said George, "with all those missiles flying. Have you any idea what's happening?"

"There have been stirrings for a few weeks, and a mob started up the hill to burn down the workhouse today. Someone read the riot act; it must have been while you were at the church. Anyway, whoever it was, we only just got him inside in time," answered Arthur.

"What happened then?" asked Robert.

"The mob went into the Red Lion to decide what to do next, and get their courage up," replied Arthur, "but we thought they would just stop there. Like the time the Yanks invaded Whitehaven, after a couple of hours in the ale house they just couldn't be bothered. Then this evening the Red Lion crowd remembered their grievances and it all started again, but the soldiers should be on their way by now."

"Soldiers don't have the choice of sitting in a nice cosy ale house and not turning out," said Robert. "But why do people feel so strongly? I didn't think anything had changed much."

"Folks want the right to vote and they still resent the enclosures," said Tom. "If we were younger and didn't have people and property to think about, we would be with them. There are always scores to settle."

"Will the womenfolk be all right? And the children?" asked Joe. "We don't have riots in Hilltop; people just do as the church and squire bid them. It makes for a quiet life."

"The women will be safe, Adam is with them and no-one will have scores to settle with him," said George. "Most of the rioters would have been taught by the old headmaster, if at all."

"Then why Arthur's window?" asked Robert.

"They will see him as part of the government because the mail coach comes here," replied Tom. "Some of the people outside aren't local, but have come from Carlisle on Robert's new railway because they enjoy the fighting. I think the Chartists are involved as well, but I am not sure what their complaint is; young Henry would know."

"We don't have many Chartists as we're too far from London. We have a few Nonconformists though, just like anywhere else," said Arthur.

"Do the Dissenters still keep themselves to themselves?" asked Joe.

"Mostly they don't mix with the church lot, but there was a mixed marriage last year; his family was church and hers was chapel. He was outside the chapel and heard her beautiful singing, and waited to meet her. It took a while as there is a lot of singing in chapels," replied Tom.

"Which services do the happy couple attend now?" asked Arthur.

"They compromised. They mostly stay home on Sundays," said Tom.

"Does Susan Graham still go to chapel?" asked Arthur.

"After the wedding fiasco she said she'd never go to church again, so she went to chapel regularly for a couple of years. Then she fell out with the Minister, who said it was unseemly for a single woman to live on her own and that people would talk," said George.

"There was no room for her in the forge after Sally's second set of twins, and she didn't fancy lodgings, so she set up home in one of her cottages," explained Tom. "She said that if anybody talked she'd have a little word with them."

George shuddered at the thought.

"To cap it all, Susan told the Minister that he was no good at running the chapel and he couldn't organize a party in an ale house," said George, "She only goes to chapel occasionally now, just when there's a visiting preacher."

"No sign of her marrying Charlie, then?" asked Joe.

"They seem to be on good speaking terms, and she has plenty of time for young Martha," answered George, "I don't see what the problem is. Even if they have worn out their welcome at church and chapel, there is still Charlie's friend the registrar; he likes doing weddings."

"Neither of them will bring up the subject of marriage, as they both see themselves as the injured party, waiting for an apology," explained Tom, "They won't budge, but a man could be carried away by a fever or hit by a paving stone tomorrow and then it's too late."

"Life is short," said George. "All we have is today." He coughed into his handkerchief, and Tom knew that he was spitting up bright red blood.

"It's all any of us have," said Tom. "Drink up and I will get another jug."

***

It was midday the following day before the brothers left the ale house, having finally worn out their welcome with Arthur. By then the soldiers had taken the troublemakers and the missiles had been cleared up from the streets so there would be no further disturbance.

Old John Harrison had the distinction of the longest wake in living memory.

21 THE PRACTICE

Charlie looked out of the window; the autumn sun was beginning to struggle through, lighting up the clouds in front of it. The previous winter had been terrible, dark, cold, windy and wet. Many of the old people and infants had been carried off by fevers, and there was nothing he and Tom could do about it. Sally had lost one of her baby twins, but the other one seemed to be picking up, after a few anxious moments. The summer had been hot and humid, with cholera taking children and adults alike.

The town was not as prosperous as it had been; the mills had big orders to supply cloth for army uniforms in the past but the country was at peace now. With the French wars, and the Regent changing his mind about the uniforms every five minutes, the mills had done very well. But now times were harder, and more of the mill workers were on short time, so there was less money to buy cloth and keep the mills going. And less money for food, so the people were weaker and had less fight in them when disease struck.

Charlie watched the sky and thought about the glimmer of hope. There had been a surprisingly good harvest, and a supper was planned at the Queen's Arms, after the annual quoits match against Hamish's team. But Charlie knew they would struggle to get a team together this year

***

When he was talking to Kit in the forge kitchen later that day, Charlie found that the situation was worse than he thought.

"I just don't think we've enough players. We have lost Gaffer and his brother and Adam says that there are no youngsters coming on now," said Kit.

"The ague took the old men, and the cholera took a couple of promising youngsters," said Charlie, "but surely we can find someone."

"You and I, Adam, George and Arthur. Would Tom play?"

"I don't think that would be a good idea, as people would be hit by flying quoits and we would be patching them up all the time. What about Ox? He would bring all his friends to cheer us on. I know Ox hasn't played for a while but he used to be very good."

"Could you ask him? I wouldn't know what to say since it's been such a long time."

"Yes, I'll ask him; that makes six, we need two more. I will ask around but what about getting your two forge men to practise with the team just in case?" asked Charlie.

"Tiny is a half decent player but hadn't thought he would ever play in the team. I am not sure about his brother Curly."

Charlie smiled at the names. Tiny was well over six feet tall and Curly was bald as a coot.

"What is Curly's problem?"

"He calls himself 'Lancelot' and has taken to writing poetry."

"Must have been that night he got too close to the ale jug," said Charlie, "but a hard fought game of quoits will sort him out. I'll have a word with their mother; she'll enjoy watching them play and will make sure they turn up."

He had a mental picture of little Mrs. Padgett frog marching her boys to the green, holding each one by the ear.

"We still have no captain," said Kit, hopefully.

"I think it goes with your job," answered Charlie.

"I'm not good enough, not like Gaffer and Richard were. I just don't know what to say to folks. Can't you do it? Please?"

"I suppose so. We can't let Arthur be captain, as he would be too busy worrying about the green and trying to sell ale."

They made arrangements for the next practice and tried not to think of missing players like Gaffer, Richard and poor Benjie.

***

The first half of the practice was a shambles; they couldn't find the quoits and had to use horseshoes. Arthur sent his son Sam to say that his dad was busy and couldn't come this afternoon, then the lad hung about in the hope of having a go. George's children, Jack and Deborah, came with him to watch the practice, and little Martha trailed up after them. With Dickon, Ben, and Sally's twins (Chris and Ricky) this made rather too many children- they all got in the way, especially Martha. Charlie sat in his position as 'shower up', encouraging the players. He had Martha next to him, one arm restraining her from running on to the pitch. Martha had something to say about each of the players; this was very distracting and Charlie had trouble keeping his face straight.

Curly was trying to look pale, interesting and delicate which was very difficult for one of his build. He tried to get away with throwing underarm and Charlie had to be firm with him. Ox and Kit played a good solid game but George didn't seem to have the strength that he used to have.

Adam couldn't decide which hand he wanted to throw with; he was slightly better with his right hand that day but thought that he could unsettle his opponents with his left. This meant that spectators had to keep moving to be out of the way, and the children were even more underfoot than they would have been.

***

George was flagging by the middle of the afternoon, so Charlie called a break for the men. The lads were hoping to have a go, which gave Charlie a bit of hope for the future; perhaps Adam could train them up to play in a couple of years' time. Sally had parked the children on the doorstep with a large slice of bread and jam each, and left Deborah in charge.

This left Charlie free to coach the lads, and by the end of half an hour Dickon could throw the horseshoe all the way to the peg and Jack was not far behind. Ben and Sam did their best but were distracted by the fact that Deborah was watching, and Martha was making comments.

Charlie called everyone to him and said that his future team was coming along very well and that Jack and Dickon could practise with the men. Charlie said that he fancied a game himself, and would George mind playing as 'shower up' to encourage and advise on tactics. By this time George was exhausted after throwing the heavy quoits and happy to take a less active role and proudly watch his son. Then they had to clear the children. Chris and Ricky struggled with the heavy horseshoes but Martha was enjoying herself and the horseshoe had to be prised out of her hand. Sally came out with baby Frances under her arm, and bribed the children with more bread and jam.

This amused everybody, especially Martha's muffled comments as she watched the game with George, saying that Jack wasn't very good and that Curly threw his quoit like a girl. Charlie was secretly proud of his daughter; she seemed to have a good grasp of the game and he wondered if she would be allowed a place on the team when she was older.

***

Later practices went better, especially as Chris and Ricky were packed off to their Aunt Susan and Martha stayed at home while George and Jack sneaked off to the forge. Arthur missed one or two practices when he was busy, and George fell asleep occasionally but on the whole the team improved. They even found the quoits, as Arthur's wife, Isabella, had hidden them away in a cupboard; she must have thought that he needed to spend more time at work.

Tom turned up at the end of the last practice, when Charlie was talking tactics.

"And another thing," explained Charlie, "you may not win this year as we have a younger and less experienced team, but you must give the Scots as good a game as possible so that they think it's worth coming next year. Then we can really hammer them."

"Is Hamish still playing?" asked Tom.

"I think so, and both his sons. I don't think he has many new players," replied Kit. "Did you decide on who was to be the reserve?"

"Jack should be first reserve, as he knows the game well and has been watching it all his life," continued Charlie. "I don't think the reserves will need to play, but Dickon could stand by as second reserve just in case. Ben and Sam should come to the game to watch and learn."

"Just one more thing before you go," said Charlie. "The other team may be impolite and call you rude names."

"Surely not!" said George with a smile.

"You are expected to reply in kind, it is half the fun," said Charlie, "but please mind your language as there will be women and children watching."

"Do you think Dickon will be up to it?" asked Tom, quietly, afterwards.

"He's miles better than Ben and Sam," replied Charlie. "He has been working hard and deserves the honour, and I don't expect he will be needed."

"But won't the other team mock if they think he is slow-witted?" asked Tom.

"He bears Richard Graham's name and stature," said Charlie, "and that will give him respect, even if he doesn't speak."

"He's not simple," said Kit. "He speaks the odd word in the forge, even whispers in the kitchen if he's on his own with little Frances."

"Does he now!" said Charlie thoughtfully.

22 THE GAME

The last Saturday in September was bright, fresh and invigorating. A few leaves had fallen and crunched underfoot, there was no wind to speak of and Charlie could hear the hum of excitement in the street outside. There was a little procession of men carrying trestle tables towards the Queen's Arms, followed by small boys carrying chairs. The harvest supper was one of the two main events of the year; the food was more plentiful than at New Year and less likely to be used as missiles.

Soon there would be women and girls with baskets containing some of the food and Charlie hoped to get a glimpse of Susan. He hadn't seen her for a while, and had heard that she disapproved of her nephews' involvement in the quoits team and thought they were too young and vulnerable. But the lads were eleven and obviously enjoying themselves, and it would do Dickon good to meet other local youngsters. Charlie thought he had better keep quiet about Dickon starting to recover his speech, because the lad was not ready to be frog-marched to school just yet.

Charlie watched the women, pleased to see a plentiful supply of large baskets. There was Susan, and he hoped that she had a plate cake in her basket, the pastry so light and the fruit so sweet that he could almost taste it. But Susan did not look up at his window, instead she turned and waited for Sally to catch up. He knew what was in Sally's basket; she made the best bread in the town.

Charlie watched them until they were out of sight and went down to the kitchen, looked for last night's flagon of beer, cleared a space on the table with his arm and cut a thick uneven slice from a stale loaf. It was his first match as captain of the quoits team, but he would worry about that when the time came. Everything would be well, Dickon would not need to play and Susan would be appeased. Charlie had a good night's sleep and it was a fine day with the prospect of a good supper. What could go wrong?

Later on Charlie opened the shop, served a few customers and sent Ben out on the morning errands. It was nearly dinnertime before Tom came in wearily after a night on call. Ben had not yet brought the dinner from the pie shop so Charlie offered the remains of breakfast; Tom waved the bread away but reached for the beer. No babies due, no old people on deathbeds, not many injuries for a Friday night- Charlie wondered where Tom could have been.

"Were you called to George?" asked Charlie softly, and Tom nodded.

"He has a chill, and not enough strength to throw it off quickly. He will survive this one," replied Tom, seeing Charlie's worried look, "but he's not fit enough to play this afternoon."

"How did he take that?" asked Charlie.

"He was set to ignore me and struggle out of bed, until I said that it would give young Jack a chance to play in a real match," answered Tom. "Will he be throwing or encouraging?"

"Jack prefers to do things, rather than watch, and he has been practising his throw," said Charlie. "He would take a dim view of it if he was asked to be shower up, although he knows the game well enough to make a reasonable fist of it."

***

Charlie arrived early for the game; he was looking forward to seeing Hamish and his team again. The old man was not as active as he had been, so he played as shower up while his sons, young Hamish and 'Little Jimmy' took charge of the throwing. Charlie was pleased to see 'Awkward' and 'Troublemaker' among the team and wished he could remember their real names. Charlie, Kit, Arthur and Adam sat with their opponents, enjoying the beer, waiting for the rest of their team to arrive.

The women were trying to organize setting the tables for the food; this was fun to watch because Susan and Mrs. Padgett both had definite ideas on how it should be done and neither was prepared to compromise. Charlie looked again. Ox had arrived with his friends; the four young lads were together and he was sure Tiny and Curly would be around somewhere as it was nearly time to start warming up.

Charlie noticed a shadow falling, which turned out to be Tiny (a big man but nowhere near as wide as Little Jimmy) and he wanted a quiet word.

"Where's your brother, I haven't seen him yet?" asked Charlie.

"Shh, not so loud," said Tiny, looking to see if his mother was listening, "I had trouble waking him this morning and he doesn't look well at all. Could you come and have a look?"

Charlie went with Tiny to see what the problem was, and found Curly in the attic instead of the room he usually shared with his brother. There were pens, paper, inkbottles and books everywhere and Curly was slumped over a small writing table. Charlie lifted him up to find papers full of blots and crossings out, and something clutched in his hand.

"I don't know what that is in his hand, but he says it is something that all poets need to help them," said Tiny.

"I don't think the contents of this hip flask have helped him much," said Charlie. "We'll have to sober him up for the match. Where's the nearest horse trough?"

Curly woke up and started retching, and Tiny thoughtfully went to fetch the chamber pot from their bedroom. They eventually got Curly onto his feet, but he was still feeling very sick and wanted to take the chamber pot to the match.

Just as they were leaving the house, Mrs. Padgett arrived.

***

"So, no Curly, then?" asked Adam.

"His mother won't let him out to play," replied Charlie. "She wasn't best pleased with us but we managed to get away when she was shouting at Curly. It would have been funny, except that we need him for the match this afternoon."

Dickon proudly took his place among the rest of the team who were warming up on the green behind the Queen's Arms, but there were murmurs among the small boys who were watching.

"That lad's simple, that's why he doesn't go to school!"

"He hasn't got all his chairs upstairs!"

"Sam should be playing instead of yon daftie!"

Ben leapt to his feet to defend his brother, but Dickon simply hefted one of the quoits and looked around at the offenders who suddenly fell silent.

Charlie realized that his depleted team stood no chance of winning, but he tried to encourage them as best he could as he stood by the hob as shower up. The Scots took a while to get used to the five-pound quoits, instead of their more usual nine pounds. They were used to aiming for a pin flush with the ground eighteen yards away; eleven yards was just something and nothing.

The English pin stuck out of the ground, and players had a more tactical game with one quoit as near to the pin as possible, preferably touching or encircling it. In the Scottish game the distance of every quoit from the pin was important. Charlie realized that his current team would have a lot of work to do to play the Scottish game in the return match, but they were managing the English game quite well and won the first two games.

In the third game, while they waited for someone to fetch little Jimmy's quoit from a neighbouring street again, Hamish suggested that he throw it more gently, 'like a bunch of flowers at a wedding'.

This amused people who remembered Charlie and Susan's doomed wedding ceremony – that bunch of flowers had not been thrown gently!

"Can't be doing with these fiddly Sassenach quoits," said Little Jimmy.

"It's a game for little boys," said Troublemaker.

"The little boys beat you fair and square twelve years ago," said Charlie, as he remembered his first game when he and Kit were just twelve.

The home team narrowly won the next game but Hamish's team was getting accustomed to the English rules. The Scots went from strength to strength and won the next four games with increasing ease. Charlie looked at his team; most of them were playing really well but Jack and Dickon were beginning to tire in spite of the extra food Ben had fetched for them. This was a deciding game; if the Scots won they had the best of nine games and would win the match. The tension was rising and so were the insults.

Jack, Ox, Arthur and Kit had thrown well, in spite of Arthur's preoccupation with the supper arrangements. The other team had a bit to say about this, especially as Arthur had forgotten to take his apron off. Adam threw next; his left-handed throw landed six inches from the hob, unsettling spectators who had moved out of the way just in case.

"The Devil looks after his own," said Troublemaker as he crossed himself. Adam's throw was the best so far.

Little Jimmy got ready to throw, his large shaggy shape blocking out the sun.

"Is that a man or a Highland Cow?" whispered Sam to Ben. This was very audible in the silence, and was repeated by the crowd with much laughter.

Little Jimmy's quoits were now landing on the green, nearer and nearer to the hob. He made a great pantomime of throwing this quoit like a bunch of flowers, much to the amusement of the crowd, but it landed touching the back of the hob. If there was no better from Tiny or Dickon, then Little Jimmy had just won the match.

Tiny was prepared, quoit in hand, and Dickon stood ready for his turn.

"Does your mother know you're out?" asked Troublemaker, referring to Dickon and the other boys.

Tiny remembered about his mother and panicked, there was no sign of little Mrs. Padgett in the crowd, but he had to look carefully; just in case. This upset his concentration, and his throw went wide of the hob. Awkward stepped up for his turn, the last player for the Scottish team.

"Are you going to fall over your feet again, they're certainly big enough?" asked Charlie to everyone's amusement.

Awkward looked at his feet to make sure that they were where he thought they should be, and his throw landed well short.

Charlie looked at Dickon as he stood nervously waiting to throw. If

Dickon's throw was better than little Jimmy's they could win the current game and play a last deciding game for the match. It was not impossible, but very unlikely- Charlie wished he had arranged for someone else to play last instead of Dickon.

"Just do your best, lad, and don't worry," he said quietly, "you've played a very good game.

The home crowd had different expectations, and fell silent as they waited for Dickon to throw; you could have heard a pin drop. Dickon felt the pressure, and tried to grip his quoit tightly as he prepared to throw, but it got tangled in his shirtsleeve and landed with a thud at his feet.

Charlie had always wondered what Dickon's first words would be when he regained his speech, but the string of oaths that came out of the lad's mouth was not at all what he expected.

23 THE MEMORY

Ben had been listening to Sam explaining the game to Deborah, when he heard his brother speak for the first time in four years. In the distance he saw his Aunt Susan coming through the crowd; she had her sleeves rolled up so he knew there was going to be trouble. Luckily he knew exactly what to do, so he quietly sidled up to Dickon, took his unresisting hand, and led him away in the opposite direction to safety. They broke into a run when they were out of sight of the crowd.

***

The lads sat in the dark and quiet of the empty forge and got their breath back, and Dickon looked questioningly at Ben.

"We're not hiding from the team; Charlie won't fault you as he said you played well. We are hiding from Aunt Susan, as she'll want to wash your mouth out with soap and water; she does it to us in school sometimes. She might do it anyway, but it's best not in public," explained Ben. He hoped Dickon would feel better in familiar surroundings, and feel braver in the place where he had felt safe for the last four years.

"Aunt Susan," whispered Dickon, very quietly.

"It'll be a while before she finds us and she might forget if she is busy organising the supper," said Ben.

"We'll miss the supper," whispered Dickon.

Ben emptied his pockets and cap of bread rolls, cheese, pies and apples. The food was a little squashed but hopefully still edible. He listened carefully at the kitchen door before he went in to find them something to wash it down with, and came back with a jug of small beer.

For a while they forgot about Aunt Susan and munched contentedly, the beer was surprisingly good. Ben and Dickon eagerly took turns to drink from the large jug. Ben found his lips strangely numb and his mind a bit befuddled.

"It's like last time when we ran away to Uncle Joe," said Ben.

"When we were little," said Dickon.

"That awful day when dad lay on the ground and wouldn't move. Did he fall off the cart?" asked Ben. "And the squire's men thought that mam had…"

He felt safe saying this as they sat in the dark, not looking at each other. Ben had kept thinking about it since the day it happened, and the only possible explanation.

"They were ever so late home, I waited ages. Mam brought the cart home and dad was just lying there. She was mopping up the blood, and she kept sending me to fetch stuff," whispered Dickon.

"Then what happened?" asked Ben, though he didn't really want to know.

"Dad was standing in the yard, holding on to the cart. Mam wanted to help him walk but he said he could manage. Then he fell and wouldn't get up and the squire's men came for my mam and I just stood there, I didn't know what to do, I should have…" whispered Dickon.

"We were only seven," said Ben as he passed him the jug again. He felt so relieved that his mother had no part in his father's death even though some terrible misfortune had befallen both of them. His mother had done everything she could to care for his father but it was all to no avail, and he felt proud of his mother's memory even though he had heard that she was hanged as a criminal.

***

Later that evening Charlie and Kit found the two missing boys fast asleep in a quiet corner of the forge.

"I will hide the evidence, as they are in enough trouble already," said Charlie, picking up the empty beer jug, "and they haven' t left us any. They must have mistaken this strong stuff for small beer."

"They'll have sore heads in the morning," said Kit with a smile, "but will Dickon be able to talk normally now?"

"He'll probably whisper to people he knows if he is somewhere he feels safe, like the forge. His speech will get gradually louder, and he might start talking in the kitchen or outside just as long as there is no setback." Charlie found both boys were looking at him.

"He won't have to go to school, will he?" asked Ben.

"Would you like to go to school, Dickon?" asked Charlie and Dickon shook his head vigorously.

"I could do with him here, "said Kit, "otherwise I'll have to hire another man to do his work."

"Has he signed his indentures?" asked Charlie.

"They're here somewhere, "said Kit, ferreting through piles of debris.

"I'll lodge them with the magistrate as soon as possible," said Charlie, "I was surprised by your language today, young Dickon." He did not say impressed.

"Sorry," whispered Dickon.

"We work with horses mostly," said Kit, "and they need a very strong signal or they would never do anything. None of your pleases and thank yous."

***

Ben decided not to go for Sunday dinner at the forge that week, and rushed about the shop cleaning and tidying things, making it look as if he was very busy.

"You have dusted that shelf three times now," stated Charlie. "Is there somewhere else you are supposed to be?"

"I didn't notice how late it was," answered Ben, "I was so busy! I will have to stay here now, this Sunday, won't I?"

"Since you are in the mood for working, Dr. Tom could do with a hand to clean that back room of his," said Charlie.

"Come on in," invited Tom, "it's not as bad as it looks."

Ben gulped and entered gingerly, and tried not to notice something scurrying past him.

"Don't worry, it is probably only a spider," explained Tom.

"I think the beastie had a tail," said Ben, hesitantly.

"It must be a mouse, then," said Tom, cheerfully, "the cat's not doing her job because she is getting old and tired. It comes to us all eventually."

Ben thought that it looked a bit big for a mouse, but did not like to think of the alternative. He could see more in the little room now that Tom was cleaning the window at the top. A stream of sunshine struggled through the dust, and lit up corners that were better left alone. Tom showed Ben an area of shelf that had been cleared, and asked him to continue the work, so Ben gingerly started, trying not to disturb too much.

The room grew lighter, and Ben suddenly noticed a skeleton grinning at them from the corner. He jumped, knocking over bookshelves precariously balanced on a couple of bricks. The skeleton suddenly had nothing to lean on, and fell against the wall with an ominous rattle; Ben nearly dropped the jar he was holding.

"Careful with that jar, we pride ourselves on our leeches," said Tom as he picked up most of the skeleton. "Put it down, and hand me some string, the bread knife, and that leg bone."

Ben hunted in the kitchen, finding the string in a saucepan and the knife under a pile of papers. He wanted to stay longer in the familiar comforting kitchen, but Tom called him back.

"Those books are underfoot, you had better sort them out next, and come back to the other shelves," said Tom. "Er, last night, did your brother say anything about the incident that brought you both here?"

"He did say a bit about it," replied Ben, moving back to Tom and handing him what he needed whilst rounding the books up into piles. Ben felt more comfortable handling the books than the jars with their unpleasant little contents.

"Leg bone please," demanded Tom as he looked at the skeleton to see what was missing, "and who got home first that day?"

"Dickon was home first; it was late so he got tea ready and waited for the rest of us. He used to do that quite often, as he got hungry," replied Ben, handing over the largest bone on the pile.

"Those bits next, on top of the pile," demanded Tom, "and who arrived home after that?"

"Mam came with the cart," answered Ben. He opened a book, closed it with a bang and there were clouds of dust that sent them both coughing.

"This seems to be holding together, it only needs string where the wiring has gone," said Tom as he gave the skeleton a bit of a rattle, "and your dad?"

"He was lying on the cart, I think," replied Ben.

Bit by bit Tom reattached the skeleton and extracted the story, and Ben dusted and replaced the books.

"I think we can finish the other shelves after dinner," decided Tom. "Can you find me a book with skeletons, I need to find where all these leftover bones should go?"

***

After dinner they all enjoyed the benefit of the rediscovered bookcase: Tom was studying skeletons, Charlie had a book on fishing, and Ben had found a book for himself.

"That's a funny book for a surgeon," said Charlie.

"It has poems, like the ones at school, only longer," said Ben. "I had to copy out and learn the one about autumn but I wouldn't fancy learning some of these others."

"Quite appropriate," said Tom. "Keats was a surgeon's apprentice like you, before he became a poet. The other poets didn't like him because he wasn't a gentleman like them."

"They didn't like him because he was miserable," said Charlie, as he went into the shop to find who had rung the bell.

Ben's heart sank when he heard his Aunt Susan's voice and he stayed as still and quiet as possible so that he would not be noticed.

"Young Dickon can speak fine when he wants to. I think he's been pretending all this time and you doctors have been covering up for him. Dickon speaks in the forge but he won't speak to me when I tell him to, not to mention yesterday's incident," said Susan.

"He can speak a little now, when he feels safe, or 'in extremis'," explained Charlie, "but he had a terrible shock as a child, and we need to go slowly, not rush him."

"He should be at school; is it too late to get his indentures back from the magistrate? I think it's sneaky the way you and Kit arranged it all without telling me. I know what's best for the lad, and he needs schooling," said Susan.

"It's impossible to get the indentures back from the magistrate," Ben thought they still might be in Charlie's pocket, "and Dickon is best where he is. Kit is his master and guardian now, until he is twenty-one. When I became a surgeon's apprentice, Dr Tom and Dr Jarvis became my joint guardians instead of my nearest relative."

"Your case was quite different, your grandmother would have caused you harm, and you wouldn't have learnt your trade. Why won't Dickon speak to me? Even after I threatened him?" asked Susan. "Where's that brother of his, I need a word with him!"

"He has gone somewhere with Dr. Tom," said Charlie. "I'm not sure where they are. Dickon may need a little more schooling but it wouldn't be kind to drag him to school away from the work he loves."

"Kind! Kind! I'll give you kind!" said Susan. "Is it kind to make free with other women when you have a sweetheart waiting for you at home? You made me a laughing stock in front of the whole town!"

Tom and Ben had heard this argument many times before and they quietly moved towards the back door, picking up their fishing rods as they went.

24 - 1844 - THE APPRENTICES

Two years had passed since the memorable quoits match; Ben, Jack, Sam and Dickon were all thirteen, and they were about to start work. They considered that school was for little children like five-year-old Martha and Sally's four-year-old twins Chris and Ricky.

It was a sunny July afternoon and the lads had been picking damsons from the tree at the back of the surgery. Dickon had shaken the tree vigorously, Sam and Ben picked up the fallen fruit, and Jack had climbed the tree to gather any damsons that were left over. They decided to have an unofficial rest and test some of the fruit before anyone gave them another job to do, as the weather was hot and they felt lazy. They felt that they had reached a turning point in their lives and enjoyed the moment; the taste of the sweet sticky fruit, the birdsong, the familiar tree above them and the rooftops beyond.

"Make the most of our last day as children, we'll be working men tomorrow," said Jack. "I wouldn't fancy your work with people's insides, Ben Sawbones, and all those things in your back room give me the creeps."

"I've got used to it all now, it isn't so bad," answered Ben. He had become familiar with the room and its contents over the previous two years, and the frightening skeleton was now cheerfully called 'Yorick'.

"What about you, Jack," asked Sam, "are you still going to work in the big mill?"

"They aren't taking anyone on just now," replied Jack, "there isn't so much work for the mills now and they are sending most of it to Carlisle. I might get to go to sea after all, maybe just go to Whitehaven on the train and see if they'll have me."

"That sounds very exciting, Jack Tar, you will go to faraway places with strange sounding names. All sorts of foreign places like in books where the natives don't speak like us," said Ben. He knew that Jack had no chance of an apprenticeship. He was the ablest of the four lads but needed to earn money straight away since his father was not expected to last the winter.

"You could fall over the side of the boat, or be eaten by cannibals," said Sam, "and that would be even more unpleasant than that back room at the surgery."

"Just," put in Dickon who was still a man of few words.

"It's a great adventure, I can't wait. Us sailors have to be very brave and skilful, there is no room for mistakes," boasted Jack. "It's much more exciting than staying here and working in the ale house with your father."

"Is that what you're doing?" asked Ben. "I heard you had an apprenticeship at the draper's." He thought this was not much of a man's job at all, and felt a bit sorry for Sam.

"At least I am safe and warm and don't have to work at night," said Sam.

"The forge is warm," put in Dickon.

"I'll have my own shop before I am twenty-one," boasted Sam, "while other people are at surgeon school, burnt to a frazzle or in a native's cooking pot."

"You will be selling material and clothes, even women's underthings," said Jack. "I wouldn't like that."

Sam blushed and the other three lads laughed at the thought of their friend having to sell corsets to the townswomen.

"You'll meet girls," said Dickon enviously, which made Sam feel better.

"Hurry up and finish picking," shouted Charlie from the doorstep. "I'll show you how to make some wine if you haven't eaten all the damsons."

The spell was broken and they all trooped indoors, wondering how long it would be before the wine was ready.

***

Ben found that his life as a surgeon's apprentice was very similar to the work he did before, carrying messages and serving in the shop; familiar work but not exciting. He was surprised to find that he missed going to school. For the last year his Aunt Susan had arranged for Dickon to have private lessons with Adam Corrie on Saturday mornings. Ben had gone to keep his brother company and learn a little Latin and more natural history. He was fascinated with all Mr. Corrie's books, and even got a chance to borrow the occasional novel or poetry book.

Ben had hoped to call in the next Saturday morning to deliver a bottle of tonic to Mrs. Corrie but this week he was needed in the surgery on Saturday morning. He had to do his errands on the Friday and he got the timing wrong as school was still in session and he did not get a chance to see Mr. Corrie and borrow another book.

Ben was not sure what part he had to play in the Saturday surgery with its tooth drawing and boil lancing and was not looking forward to it.

"Come here, lad, and put this on," ordered Charlie, handing him a grubby apron. "Things could splash on you otherwise, blood, pus and the like. And it will give you something to wipe your hands on."

"Do I really have to wear an apron?" asked Ben; he had laughed at Sam in his apron earlier in the week. "I could just stand well back."

"I don't want you to stand well back, I need you to help. A surgeon's apron is an honourable garment; look at all those blood stains," said Charlie, but this did not help. "I will do the tooth drawing first, you can help Dr. Tom hold the patients down. Has your friend Jack come back from foreign parts yet? Which exotic places did he visit?"

"Yes, he has a day or two on leave, and goes back next week. He's been to strange places where the people speak a different language," said Ben, "Liverpool was bad enough but he couldn't understand a word they said in Greenock."

The first patient came in for tooth drawing, pushed by some of his friends and smelling strongly of drink. They got him into a chair, wedged it into place and Tom showed Ben how to do the proper arm lock and brace himself. Charlie flourished an evil looking set of pincers above the patient's head for the benefit of the crowd, and then removed the offending tooth remarkably quickly.

"Is that all?" asked the patient.

"I could take a few more if you like; it's all the same to me," said Charlie picking up the pincers, "any more for any more?"

A couple more men plucked up courage to have teeth drawn, but the crowd was a bit disappointed that there was no screaming and yelling that week. Tom left to visit his brother George, who had not recovered after his latest chill, and Charlie looked at the queue in the shop.

"Who's next? A splinter, a lovely big one! I'll soon pull it out for you!" said Charlie, wiping the pincers on his apron.

The carpenter's youngest came forward and had the splinter removed with no fuss, but Curly was more reluctant when it came to his turn. Tiny and Ben held Curly firmly while Charlie removed a very small splinter from his finger. Curly turned pale, and insisted on a bandage so Ben found himself bandaging the finger and keeping his face straight when he listened to some of the crowd's comments.

There were a couple of men in the queue who had been injured in a fight the night before but hadn't noticed until the morning. Charlie was making short work of the cleaning, stitching and iodine and Ben noticed there was only one quivering patient left among the people who stayed to watch the fun. He recognized the lad from school, Crusher, a bully who terrorized the smaller children.

"What is the matter with you?" asked Ben, feeling very bold.

"Dr. Charlie's going to lance my boil," said Crusher quietly.

"Where is the boil?" asked Ben innocently although he knew that Crusher was one of the registrar's clerks and spent a lot of time sitting down. Crusher told him once, and Ben told him to speak louder as he didn't hear; he wanted all the audience to know exactly where it was.

"Will it hurt much?" asked Crusher.

"It'll hurt a lot but it has to be done. We know somebody whose foot fell off because he had a boil that festered," explained Ben who was beginning to enjoy himself.

"Next please," shouted Charlie as Crusher was pushed forward.

The screens were drawn so the crowd missed seeing the delicate operation, but they did not miss the yells when Charlie lanced the boil or the louder yells when Ben applied the iodine. On the whole Ben thought that the morning's surgery had been very satisfactory.

***

After dinner, Martha arrived with a message to say that Dr. Tom was going to be back later than expected from visiting her foster father George. She hung around and asked if she could help, so she was sent on one or two errands while Ben helped Charlie to restock the shop shelves with medicines, pills and potions ready for the next week.

Martha was fascinated with the shop and the medicines, but most of all she liked to be taken to the back room to see Yorick and the jar of leeches. She invited herself to tea, and proved a welcome diversion as she amused Charlie by discussing the local school with Ben; she had all the latest gossip and strong opinions on what was going on. Martha was in no hurry to return so Charlie had to stand holding her coat in front of her before she reluctantly made a move.

Later in the evening Charlie and Ben were in the kitchen, making up medicines and pills to last them through the next week. The nights were drawing in and people would want cough remedies, tonics and ointment for chilblains in addition to the usual treatments for cuts, bruises and delicate digestive systems. They were still trying to ignore the noise of the people outside when Sam came to tell them that they were needed and would they please hurry up.

25 THE FIRE

Susan heard the noise outside her house, opened the door, and found the street unexpectedly smoky, as if it were bonfire night. It was darker than usual for the time of evening, but she could see people hurrying towards the direction the smoke was coming from. Susan thought there must be a house on fire, which was not unusual, and automatically followed the crowd in the hope that she could help the victims. The heat hit her when she turned the corner, and she realized that the situation was more serious.

The town's biggest mill was ablaze, the heat was fierce and the smoke suffocating. Susan could see the skeleton of the building against the flames, and realized that nothing could be saved, no people, machinery, cloth or cotton, not even the building. People stood in disbelief; the mill had been there as long as anyone could remember and now it was gone. There was a collective moan each time part of the roof fell in.

At first it looked as if no one was doing anything useful, but she found a group of familiar people near the horse trough, helping the victims. Some people had found the smoke too much, and were struggling to breathe so Dickon, Curly and Tiny were taking them home in wheelbarrows away from the heavy smoke. Arthur's wife, Isabella, was rounding up the walking wounded to take them to the ale house out of the way, so that they did not add to the number of smoke victims. Adam Corrie and Sam Brown were helping her nephew Ben deal with minor burns; she thought that dipping hands in the horse trough was a bit unorthodox but it seemed to work. But where were Tom and Charlie?

"Was there…is there any one still in there?" asked Susan, but surely there couldn't be.

"The shift had finished, there was only the night watchman who raised the alarm, but Kit and Charlie have gone to make sure," answered Adam.

"They haven't gone…in there?" asked Susan; surely they couldn't have.

She felt a lump in her throat at the thought of her brave Charlie going to the rescue, and was terrified that he might be in danger. She hadn't realized how much she still cared, and tried to suppress the urge to rush after him.

"I don't think so," said Adam, "they went to see the foreman and the overlookers from the last shift, so they could make sure that everyone was accounted for. The mill owners are away in Carlisle, and nobody else thought to do it. Charlie set us on, treating the injured, and then went to make sure nobody was still inside."

"So nobody has been brought out? Which injuries are you treating?" asked Susan; she was so proud of her Charlie, caring enough to think of the victims, but going about it in an organized way. Not just standing about in a daze like everybody else. But could he be irresponsible enough to risk his life going into the mill if he thought someone might be trapped? Surely nobody could live in those flames and he would be risking his life for nothing. She fought back the wave of panic. Charlie was known to be irresponsible in the past and he had lied to her.

"These are just people who stood too near the fire, because they wanted a good look," replied Adam, "the burns are superficial."

"Is there anything I can do?" Susan asked Adam although Ben appeared to be in charge.

Ben and Adam looked at each other, but it was Sam that spoke.

"You could go and ask the people to stand further back, miss," he suggested, "It would make our work a lot easier. My father keeps trying to tell them but they won't listen to him."

They will listen to me all right, thought Susan, and as she hurried along, she saw Charlie and Kit striding back, both faces grim. She was overwhelmed with relief, but she did not want him to see her weakness; the words left her mouth and she could not call them back.

"So you are back at last, I am surprised at you, leaving children to do your work at a time like this," she said, and regretted it straight away. She wanted to just run into his arms and hold him, but everyone was watching. She had a job to do and needed to keep her authority with the crowd.

***

It wasn't until afterwards that Susan realized that she had not seen Tom, or any of his brother George's family. Susan was fond of Jeannie, who had been a close friend of Nancy's years ago. Now Susan thought she was getting maudlin, she had tried not to think about Nancy for years, so she gathered up some bread and a few goodies and went round to Jeannie's.

Jack opened the door as Jeannie and her mother-in-law, Sarah, were just sitting, their arms around each other, stony faced, hiding their tears. Deborah was sobbing quietly, young Martha was asleep in the corner, oblivious to it all. The fire had gone out and nobody had noticed. Susan thought that this was not the time to wade in and take over so she just put the basket down gently on the table.

She jumped when she saw George come downstairs; he still looked gaunt but had put back some of the weight he had lost. Then she realized that the man coming down the stairs was Tom; he was there as a doctor as well as a brother.

"Jeannie, mother, children, it won't be long now- I think you had better come up now and say your goodbyes," suggested Tom quietly.

Susan wondered how many other families had similar news from Tom over the years, and now it was his own family. She saw how worn out he looked, and thought how hard it must be for him.

"You go, Jeannie," said Sarah, "I'll look after Martha for you."

"You both go," said Susan, picking up the sleeping child. "I'll see to Martha."

The child in her arms looked so peaceful, she could not believe she was the same lovable lively hoyden who kept Elizabeth busy in the school infant class. Martha had the same hooked nose and thick black hair as Charlie, also the same blue eyes and charm when she was awake. It was funny how features that made a man very attractive, did no favours for a woman. The squint had not come to anything so Martha might marry after all, if she could overcome her nature and become more amenable as she grew older. Susan's first thought was to take Martha to Sally's house, as one more child would not make any difference in that kitchen, but she changed her mind and took the child to her own home instead.

***

The day of George's funeral had seemed very long to Susan as she helped Jeannie with the preparations and the funeral tea. Now the last of the visitors had gone, Deborah had gone to bed worn out with weeping and Mary Ann had taken her mother home. The two women sat in companionable silence in the candlelight waiting for Jack to return, Jeannie sewing as always.

"I always wondered why women don't go to the funeral ceremony," said Susan, "surely they don't expect that we would just weep and wail and be undignified."

"Poor Mrs. Harrison would find it hard to keep the tears under her control, as George was her favourite," answered Jeannie, "and that could just set everybody off."

"I can understand why young girls stay at home, but why are lads like my nephews expected to go?"

"Jack will represent me, and it is good that his friends are with him. He is a man now, doing a man's job as a sailor. He'll have seen more of the world in his short time as a deckhand than you and I'll see in a lifetime. He's the man of the house now, but I expect he'll look to Dr. Tom for advice."

"I always thought that he would have worked in the mill like his father and grandfather," said Susan, but she did not say that the sea was a dangerous place.

"The mill owners weren't taking on workers at the time, and Jack got the chance to go to sea. George and Dr. Tom thought it was a good idea, and it will get it out of his system. Now there's no big mill and a lot of families will go hungry this winter."

"The owners will rebuild the mill, surely. The people in this town would struggle without it."

"I don't know," said Jeannie, slowly, "I've heard rumours that they might not, as there is not as much demand for calico as there was. Their best workers have been asked to go to one of the Carlisle mills, but it could be just until trade picks up."

"What will happen, without the big mill?" Susan, was thinking of all the children in the top class who were expecting to be working in the mill next year.

"Jack has his keep and sends money home. I will earn my living with my needle as best I can," said Jeannie, who had been thinking about the future during the long nights sitting up with George, "but Deborah may have to go into service. My children will look after me if necessary, but who will look after you? Has Charlie done something so unforgivable that you'll never marry him? You aren't getting any younger."

Susan still thought of herself as a young girl, as she was six years previously, and hadn't noticed the passage of time. People would think she was on the shelf, at her age with no husband or child. Men were different, and could marry at any time and Charlie seemed to be surrounded by children. Martha was one of Susan's favourite children, but she could not imagine setting up home with Charlie and bringing up his lovechild from another woman. Susan put these thoughts to one side and turned the conversation to safer talk on the fashion for caps rather than bonnets.

26 THE ILLNESS

Tom must be tired after George's illness and the funeral, thought Charlie as he saw him with his brothers and Mary Ann's husband, Henry. Tom looked a lot older than his two brothers, but Joe had been the eldest by two years. The carpenter and the registrar were in his group by the ale house fire; Hamish and his sons were still there although the rest of the quoitsmen had gone.

Jack's friends surrounded him; Charlie and Adam were teaching the four young lads to play billiards with varying degrees of success. Dickon spent his day dealing with great big lumps of metal so he found billiards very fiddly and was nervous of breaking the cue or tearing the cloth. Ben was playing a solid, competent game but his mind seemed to be elsewhere - that was how he seemed to live his life, he went through the motions and got things done but nobody knew what went on in his head.

Sam talked a much better game than he played, but Charlie thought that might be a good skill to have, as it would always help him get by and make the best of things. All the lads were learning - as long as they didn't copy Adam when he played with his left hand - but Jack was the real star. He was unusually deft for a Harrison, and his excellent balance had improved still further by climbing the rigging at sea, so he was a natural billiards player.

Jack's eyes shone; he was really enjoying himself as he mastered his new skill, so much that he almost forgot why he was there, which was what Charlie was hoping for. Charlie also thought that if Jack got a taste for billiards it would slow down his drinking at foreign ale houses, his money would last longer and he might even make a little more.

Charlie had Jack and Dickon on his team; Adam had Ben and Sam, so that the teams were very closely matched. The last game was so exciting that the lads did not want their play to finish but had no choice when Kit threatened to take them home in the wheelbarrow. Sam was already at home in his father's ale house and would have hung around, but when Arthur suggested that he clear some of the pots, he suddenly found that he was tired.

The young energetic lads left. Charlie and Adam joined the older men, and tried not to think about the passage of time. Tom coughed, Charlie looked around sharply, but it was Hamish that spoke.

"You've changed since I saw you last, Dr. Tom, you used to fill out that waistcoat and now there's nothing of you!" said Hamish.

"People said I filled out the waistcoat rather too much. I was losing buttons all the time with no-one to sew them on," replied Tom.

"Are you missing those meat pies you used to like?" asked Hamish.

But Charlie knew that the household was still keeping the pie shop busy, and that Tom was looking decidedly peaky. He hadn't noticed earlier, as he saw Tom every day, but now Hamish had pointed it out, and there was a worrying cough.

"I think you have been working too hard, Tom, and need a rest. A few weeks staying with me in Hilltop, enjoying that wonderful mountain air will soon blow all those cobwebs away," said Joe. "Not that I think there's anything wrong with you but I could use a bit of company."

"I couldn't possibly leave the practice for all that time," argued Tom. "I have a responsibility to the town and my colleagues." He remembered Joe making a similar offer to George in the past and he had made excuses too.

"The churchyards are full of indispensable people," said the registrar. "Physician, heal thyself."

"We are surgeons, rather than physicians," said Charlie, "so we have more common sense. But while there's no big mill we will not be treating so many accidental injuries - there will just be the usual fighting on Saturdays. Ben and I can manage, and Martha is fairly reliable at running errands."

"Thunderbolt would struggle with the journey these days," said Tom, not saying that he didn't fancy the long horseback ride either.

"I am going back by the afternoon train, so you needn't trouble Thunderbolt," pleaded Joe, "you've plenty of time to make up your mind."

***

All Charlie's practical arguments could not persuade Tom to go to Hilltop, but he found several Harrisons waiting outside the shop the next morning; they squeezed into Tom's kitchen and all had good reasons for Tom to take Charlie's advice. Joe explained that the farm workers of Hilltop were much healthier than the mill workers in his home town, and lived out full lives of fifty or sixty years. Sarah Harrison had tears in her eyes; her son George had been a mill worker and he had died at the age of thirty-five.

Elizabeth, with help from Adam, reminded everyone that her life had been saved by a winter in Hilltop several years previously, and Sarah started weeping softly. Robert said that he did not want to be trailing back home for another funeral too quickly and Sarah's sobs got louder and louder with Elizabeth and Mary Ann joining in.

Charlie could see that Tom was wavering. Henry raised his voice to offer help with family responsibilities in Tom's absence, whatever the outcome. Joe shouted over the noise that he expected Tom to meet him on the station platform that afternoon, and would fetch him if necessary.

Tom collapsed weakly on a chair and capitulated, and Charlie gratefully shooed the visitors out of the shop.

"How do you feel now?" asked Charlie, moving forward to take his pulse.

"Very tired, so perhaps I do need a rest," said Tom, moving out of range, "but there is something I need to do first. Nancy gave me a letter for her boys and I promised to deliver it when they were grown up. I would have kept the letter a year or two longer, but I will hand it over now, just in case I perish in the frozen wastes of Westmorland."

"I could give them the letter when the time came," said Charlie, "you have no need to worry. Is it among these papers, somewhere?"

He started looking through the papers on the cluttered table, thinking that maybe Tom was right and the boys should have the letter unless it was already lost. Perhaps Nancy would explain in the letter exactly what had happened to Benjie, and why she had been taken to jail.

Ben came out of the backroom where he had been hiding from the noisy Harrisons, but he was fully aware of what was going on. Eventually Tom unlocked a small bureau hidden behind a fire screen and under a pile of books, and triumphantly produced an envelope addressed to Ben and Dickon.

The contents were a lock of hair and a short letter. It took a while for Ben to read the words; the handwriting was excellent but had faded over the years so it took him a while to make it out. Ben sat on a stool, as near to the window as possible. Charlie gave the window a wipe with a grimy cloth but it did not help much. Ben seemed very young to cope with such news on his own, but Charlie did not want to read the letter without permission – although he had been prepared to secretly steam it open some years earlier.

Ben quietly handed the letter to Tom, and indicated that Charlie should read it as well before they went to the forge to see his brother Dickon.

***

They arrived at the forge to find that dinner was nearly ready; a fuss was made of the new arrivals, extra bread and ham was fetched, more chairs were found for the table, and Charlie suddenly realized that he was hungry.

It wasn't until afterwards, when the little ones were having their afternoon nap, that Sally took another look at her visitors and asked if there was anything wrong.

"I'm visiting my brother in Hilltop for a week or so," said Tom, not mentioning his illness, "but there is something I need to do first. Last time I saw your sister Nancy she gave me a letter, and asked me to give it to her sons when they were older. It may not make easy reading at any age. Ben has read the letter and I have brought it for Dickon to read."

Tom produced the letter for Dickon. Kit and Sally slowly nodded but Susan tried to take the letter from him.

"I think they are far too young to understand, and should wait until they are twenty-one before reading the letter," argued Susan.

"They are doing men's work now," replied Tom, handing the letter to Dickon. "Ben has already read the letter so it is only right that Dickon should do so."

Dickon went over to the open door so that he could see better, and stood, frowning, one hand holding the letter, the other one trying to trace the words on the first line.

"It is all in joined up writing, it may take a time for me to read it," said Dickon apologetically.

"The writing is a bit faint," said Ben, "and I might have missed bits."

"I told you that they were too young, we shouldn't be troubling their heads with it," said Susan. "Nancy might upset them with what she's written."

"Maybe so, but they're entitled to know. The letter tells us what we already suspected," said Tom, "and Ben has already shown it to us."

"It was very difficult to read," said Ben, as Dickon seemed to be still struggling, "it took me ages and the light was better then."

"Shall I write it out for you," said Sally, "and read it to you as I go along? Then you each will have a copy to keep."

Dickon handed her the letter gratefully, and she read it out as she printed in large clear letters for him.

Whitehaven Jail

September 1838

My Darling Boys

It breaks my heart that I will never see you again, never see you grow into the fine young men you promise to be. Tomorrow justice will be done and my life will come to an end. I had no intentions of causing harm but a man has died because of me and I will pay the penalty.

I am making my peace with God and Man. I can no longer have your father's forgiveness but I ask you for yours. It must be hard to lose both parents but you are among friends and family far away from the place of our troubles.

Do not cry for me, I have lived my life and would not want to be here any longer without your father. Work hard (Dickon blushed as he remembered avoiding his writing lessons) **and behave well** (Ben was worrying if his mother could have caused his father's death, and even though it seemed unlikely after what Dickon had told him earlier, it was by far the worst way to be orphaned) **for your godfathers and aunts; I shall look down and be proud of you.**

Your loving mother

By the end of the letter Sally was in tears and Susan had turned away to hide hers. Kit was visibly shaken.

"So both our parents are dead, then," said Dickon in a wobbly voice as he thought again about his mother dying a criminal's death at the end of a rope.

"You will always have family here," soothed Sally, kindly, "and your parents would be proud of you both."

***

Ben appeared to be lost in thought, as they helped Tom pack and make his way to the station. Charlie had altered the clock to make sure they were at the station on time, with the result that they arrived five minutes earlier than Joe and ten minutes earlier than the train. Tom was looking up and down the platform, rather surprised at all the bustle. Ben seemed lost in thought as usual.

"Penny for your thoughts, young Ben," said Charlie.

"I wondered if I would be allowed to ride Thunderbolt while Dr. Tom is away - just to exercise him, like," said Ben.

"I see no problem, just don't get too fond of riding Thunderbolt as I shall need him when I return," replied Tom. It must be hard for the lad; he had just read the letter from his mother that reminded him that he was an orphan, now his godfather was poorly, and might not come back from his travels. "After the letter you read, are there any questions you would like to ask?"

"I know my mother will be buried inside the prison, but has my father a grave where I could remember them both?" asked Ben, and Tom promised to find out as much as he could about Benjie Armstrong's last resting place.

27 THE FELLS

Tom had one or two train journeys to Carlisle in the past, but was always struck by how busy the station was. There were the passengers, waiting for the train - the town's dignitaries waited where the second-class carriage was expected to arrive. They were guaranteed wooden seats in their carriage and a roof to shelter them from the worst of the weather but not necessarily windows to keep out the driving rain. Tom felt that he and Joe could socially justify travelling in second-class but Joe resented paying the extra money when third-class would get them home just the same.

Third-class varied; sometimes there were seats, but it was no worse than travelling on a cart, on top of the mail coach or on Thunderbolt (especially on Thunderbolt). Travelling was always going to be uncomfortable, noisy and messy- it was just a question of getting it over with, and the train driver was unlikely to get lost. The first-class passengers had plush seats, windows and warm waiting rooms. Joe said that it was a waste of money and no wonder the upper class were soft.

Tom looked at the other people on the platform. His family was there to make sure he got on the train. An important looking man in a top hat and smart coat stood proudly on the platform, there was an official looking clerk in the booking office, uniformed porters hovering near the waiting rooms, young lads were sweeping the platform and older men were ready to load parcels on to the train. There was even a left luggage office where the gentry could leave their belongings for their servants to pick up later.

Men in dirty overalls were ready in case they were needed, and there was even a man with flags ready to wave the train off. It seemed like a lot of people trying to look busy in front of the stationmaster; it was not like the good old days when the horses and one drunken coachman had done all the work. Tom looked at the magnificent stone building that had been built for the station, and compared it to the cosy ale house where the coaches stopped – now there was a convenient place to wait for transport.

The train arrived amid great excitement; wheels were tapped, coal was loaded and the parcels travelled second class with one of the men in uniform. Tom and Joe were herded into the third-class truck; they squeezed into a corner as far from the livestock as possible. Tom was grateful that the carriage was open as the smell would have been unbearable.

It seemed an age before they arrived at Hilltop, cold, aching and glad that the journey was over. The platform looked deserted except for a man in a shabby uniform who unloaded some of the parcels, and waved the train off. There was no big stone building, just a tin roofed wooden hut as a shelter from the weather. The hut seemed to serve for several purposes; the stationmaster checked the tickets and asked if they needed to leave anything in the left luggage office, which appeared to be under his desk, next to his sweeping brush.

The evening was dark and cold, so Tom was pleased to spend the rest of it at the cosy inn where Joe worked, and it was good to know that he would get a good night's rest without being interrupted. For the first few days the weather was cold and wet, the sky dark, and Tom just felt like sitting by the fire and resting, as he was still coughing and that made him tired; he hoped he was not being grumpy but he couldn't even think straight.

The next day the sun shone and he felt better so he wrapped himself up warmly and set off for a walk. Tom thought the weather was very cold, but Joe was in shirtsleeves and saying that it was like the height of summer there. Tom noticed that the fields and buildings of the tenant farmers seemed more neglected than on his last visit; the barn that had been Nancy's prison had fallen down and become a heap of wood that nobody had bothered to pick up.

Tom took a circular route and came back via the church, which was in need of repair and had an overgrown churchyard. He went into the churchyard, as this was the most likely place for Benjie to be buried. He did not expect to see a headstone, and was reading the names on the little wooden crosses when he felt that he was being watched.

"Are you looking for any one in particular?" Tom turned to see an old man peering over his spectacles at him.

"A kinsman of mine," his godson's father was a kinsman, surely, "Benjie Armstrong, he died here in September 1838. Do you know where he is buried?"

"I'm sexton here, so I should know where everybody ended up, but I don't rightly remember. That was the time the old squire died, and he is sorely missed," said the sexton, looking at the state of the church and churchyard.

"Is there any way you could find out?" asked Tom. "I should like to pay my respects."

"Come back tomorrow when I've had a look at the records," answered the sexton. "I should be able to let you know where your kinsman is buried, if he's here at all. You aren't from these parts, are you?"

"I'm here for my health," said Tom, as the wind whistled over the graveyard and the sky threatened snow.

"It's a funny place to visit for your health," said the sexton. "I will look out for you tomorrow."

***

The next day the sexton was even less forthcoming, and said that he thought an incomer had died at the same time as the old squire, but there was no record of a burial so perhaps his kinfolk had taken him. Tom knew that was not the case, and when he had tried the other churches without success he decided that it was time for a talk with his brother.

He cornered Joe after the ale house customers had gone home, and suggested that they have a drink and pipe together, like in the old days.

"Is it going to end up at three o'clock in the morning with both of us under the table?" asked Joe as he filled a large jug.

"I hope so," said Tom, and Joe's eyes lit up.

Tom decided to broach the subject after the first two drinks, and pace himself a little after that, so that he could remember what was said.

"I had a look at the church the other week and got talking to the sexton," he said, pouring Joe some more ale.

"Funny old man, but nothing gets past him."

"He couldn't find any record of Benjie Armstrong's burial, and the other churches were the same."

"It's strange that there was no funeral, he must have been buried privately somewhere," said Joe, "we're still too wary of the powers that be, so nobody asked."

"The sexton seems to miss the old squire: who's in the big house now?"

"The squire's second son, Mr. Peregrine, is there now with his wife, but they are away a lot; he sacked the estate manager and doesn't bother with the place much."

"And the old squire's wife?" asked Tom, "does she still live there?"

"Milady hides away in the dower house; it's a very sad story. When she married the squire she wouldn't have anything to do with her friends and family, and thought she was too good for them. Now they don't have any time for Milady anymore," said Joe, "and I can't say that I blame them."

"Doesn't Mr. Peregrine look after his mother?" Tom felt that Milady could answer a few questions if she had a mind to.

"Milady was lady's maid to his late mother before she married the squire. Mr Peregrine and his brother thought the marriage was a bit quick after the funeral, and they didn't like taking orders from a former servant.

They only did what they had to and they thought the squire's death was partly Milady's fault."

"The squire died about the same time as Benjie Armstrong, didn't he?" asked Tom, asking Joe's daughter Sadie for another jug of ale.

"I knew you would get on to that. Nobody really knows what happened that day so it is no good plying me with more ale because I can't tell you anymore."

"Some of us know a bit more about it," said Sadie as she carried over the jug. She was a well-built girl of about fifteen who carried herself as if she knew everything.

"You're far too young to know anything."

"I know more than you think, and I know that Milady is no better than she should be," retorted Sadie. "I knew what she was up to with Mr. Armstrong."

"You can't possibly know, you were only a child at the time and you're not much older now."

"Milady was in the hayloft with Mr. Armstrong, and the squire caught them at it."

"You should not spread rumours like that."

"What else can you do with them?" she asked, dodging away from her father's hand, "anyway it's not a rumour, Jem was there at the time."

"You see far too much of that Jem, people will talk," reproved Joe, "anyway, he would have been too young to understand anything he saw."

"What did Jem see, Sadie?" asked Tom softly, wedging his foot under Joe's to stop him sliding under the table.

"He needed hay for the horses and he saw them all under the hayloft. Mr. Armstrong was on the floor, covered in blood, out cold," said Sadie, "and Mrs. Armstrong had her sleeves rolled up and a pitchfork in her hand; he could see that she meant business. The squire sort of crumpled up and fell, and didn't get up, so Jem ran for help. Jem was only nine; there was nothing else he could have done."

"And what happened then?" asked Tom, as Joe's eyes glazed over.

"Jem came back with Mr. Percy and Mr. Peregrine, and all the other men came running. They saw the squire on the ground. Mrs. Armstrong had gone but they soon found her and took her to jail."

"And Milady?" asked Tom.

"Fainted, apparently," said Sadie, "very convenient. Nobody saw her for months."

"It's all gossip; only three people saw what really happened and they are all dead," said Joe, making one last effort before he slid under the table in spite of Tom's best efforts.

***

Tom slept badly that night, thinking about Nancy. Had she killed Benjie with her pitchfork? He found it difficult to believe that she could have killed him or the squire but what if the squire was threatening Benjie, and she thought his life was in danger? She had always been a big girl; she did not know her own strength, and there had been a similar incident once before.

If Nancy killed the squire in Benjie's defence she would never get a fair trial in these parts. A rich man could ruin a poor man because he could afford better lawyers and he knew his way round the legal system. Could it have been an accident? If it was an accident, or self-defence, then she was convicted unfairly. Was there anything that Tom could have done? But when he saw Nancy she was convicted with no chance of an appeal, and she told him nothing about the incident. She said she felt responsible for a man's death, but what did she really mean? And a pitchfork looked very deliberate; you didn't mess about with those, but Dickon had said that Nancy was trying to treat Benjie's wounds when he last saw her.

In the morning Tom had a thumping headache as he joined a bleary eyed Joe at the breakfast table, so there was not much conversation. Tom decided to write to Charlie with the information he had found so far, leaving it up to him how much he passed on to the lads. Having drawn a blank on Benjie's last resting place he would write to Mary Ann's husband, Henry, to see where Nancy was buried just in case it was outside the prison.

By the afternoon Tom felt much better, and thought that he might go home in a day or two, after he had a reply from Henry. Perhaps he would have one last try at finding some information from the workhouse; he would offer his services as a doctor, in the hope of seeing the old records. It was still possible that Benjie was treated and buried there in a pauper's grave.

***

The workhouse master said that they had their own doctor, and didn't need Tom's services. However, they changed their minds the next day, as the snow had fallen early that year and many of their staff were marooned in the neighbouring village. In the weeks before the snow lifted Tom had plenty of time to examine the records, but there was no information about Benjie.

When the first train was able to get to Hilltop Tom had still not received his long delayed letter from Henry, but decided it was time to go home. He was feeling and looking much better, and no longer coughing. Joe saw him on to the train, pleased that Tom's health had improved and convinced that the cold healthy air was responsible.

28 THE BASKET

The school was closed for a week at the start of Lent, giving the children a chance to help their parents with the lambing, or preparing the fields for sowing. Susan always looked forward to her winter break from school; she usually had a rest, caught up with her chores and went back refreshed. It had been a very hard winter, and it would be another six weeks before the grass started growing for the cows to give milk again and for the hens to start laying. Frugal housewives knew to eke out their stores at this time of year, but there were always some families who had to go into the workhouse.

Susan took the opportunity to visit Jeannie, she enjoyed her restful company and liked to help with some of the more straightforward sewing, but this time she found Jeannie in her big pinafore and with her sleeves rolled up, giving the house a major spring clean.

Deborah's room was having an extra good turn out this year and Susan wondered why the work was suddenly necessary and how Deborah had escaped her share of it. Jeannie had tidied the cupboard, so she had a pile of things to throw out or give away. She was putting some baby clothes to one side, shedding a tear or two as she thought of the passage of time, the baby she lost, and her future as a widow with no more children. Susan tried not to notice the tears, and threw herself into the activity of dusting the shelves and putting fresh paper on them.

"I am glad you're here, Susan. I need a bit of help with this bed."

The bed that Deborah and Martha shared was large and heavy and looked as if it had not been moved for years.

"It seems early for spring cleaning," said Susan as she moved the rug out to the landing. "I expected to help you with sewing."

"I've no sewing this week, but might have some in a few days. Trade has been slow since the fire; so many people went to work in the other mill in

Carlisle and the people left don't want new clothes. So I thought I'd give the rooms a good turn out while I had the time."

The two women tried to heave the side of the bed away from the wall.

"Surely things will pick up."

They slowly walked the bed towards the middle of the room. Susan tried not to look down at what was under the bed as that was Jeannie's problem.

"I'm looking for a smaller house now to save on rent. I'm trying to get rid of clutter, but when Jack visits he brings things back from his travels, and it's never anything useful. He's been to America, and will go to New South Wales next time."

Susan was going to ask what was new about South Wales, when she kicked a very solid object. She looked down quickly, hoping it was not a chamber pot. Among the dust and odd socks was a basket containing a very disgruntled looking cat, which hissed at her.

"So that's where Martha's basket got to!" said Jeannie as she turfed out the cat and picked up the basket. "Off you go and have your kittens somewhere else! The girls must have had their dolls in this basket and forgotten about it - it needs a good clean before I put it away with the layette. The baby clothes had beautiful soft material, fine delicate stitching and expensive lace but I don't think they were new. I had better give this basket a clean before I put them all away."

"Can't you sell it all?" asked Susan as she picked up the rug.

"It's not mine to sell. I will look after it for Martha until she decides what to do with it."

Susan took the rug into the yard, hung it over the clothesline and beat it mercilessly, thinking about Charlie for some reason. She was really enjoying herself and didn't notice when Jeannie came out to say that she had found a letter in the basket lining.

"For Charlie, from his fancy woman, I suppose," grumbled Susan, taking her frustrations out on the helpless rug.

"That's the thing, it's very strange. The writing has faded but it seems to be addressed to 'Benjie's cousin.' I will ask Deborah to take it round when she gets back."

"That's all right. I am going this evening to …er…see my nephew, I can take the letter then."

***

The rest of the day went slowly, but Susan did not want to take the letter too early when Charlie was out on his rounds. She wanted to wait until the shop was closed for the evening, and there was no risk of Charlie putting it to one side because he was busy. Ideally she would try to find the hour when Ben was tidying the shop, but before Charlie was likely to get called out on evening visits.

Susan looked at the writing again, a woman's hand but no better than the girls in her class. And the letter was addressed to 'Benjie's cousin' so it must have been someone that Charlie met when he visited his cousin in Hilltop. At least they would know who Martha's mother was, and she could ask questions about her. But Jeannie said the baby clothes were exquisite - and she should know - so where could a countrywoman from Westmorland have got them?

Susan arrived at the shop, Ben showed her through to the kitchen and made himself scarce for some reason, but he always seemed to avoid her if he could. She handed the letter to Charlie, sat down, took her hat off and waited. Charlie offered tea if she would like to pour it, so Susan took her time boiling the kettle and refreshing the pot so that Charlie would have plenty of time to read the letter. He put the letter down and sat in a daze, ignoring the cup of tea in front of him.

"That letter must have been from Martha's mother," said Susan who was itching to just pick it up and read it. She wished she had given way to her instincts and steamed it open, earlier on.

"Well, who is she?" asked Susan, as Charlie did not answer. "You must know!"

"I've no idea," replied Charlie, absently.

"Which trollop did you seduce when you visited Benjie?" asked Susan. "Are you telling me there were several? She didn't even know your name!"

"My virtue was never compromised when I visited Benjie," answered Charlie slowly. "Martha isn't my daughter."

"She must be, she's the image of you," accused Susan, trying not to mention his late unlamented grandmother.

"Read it for yourself," capitulated Charlie, handing her the letter.

While Susan's mouth was denying that she would ever stoop to read anyone else's private letter, her hands were grabbing it eagerly before he could change his mind.

`To Benjie's cousin and next of kin`
`You must look after Benjie's baby. She looks`
`so much like him and not like me. I dare not keep`
`her here, she is noisy and I cannot hide her`
`anymore. She is obviously not my husband's child.`
`I would be thrown out.  I would rather die than`
`go into the workhouse.`

Now it was Susan's turn to ignore her tea and stare blankly in front of her.

"It's a strange letter, isn't it?" asked Charlie, breaking the silence. "Martha's mother sounds very frightened."

"The letter sounds as if she is making Benjie and his family responsible for the baby," said Susan, "much too inconvenient for the mother to look after her."

"I have delivered scores of babies, and there were not many that were 'convenient', but most of them were loved in spite of it," added Charlie, "but this one…"

"Women are practical people, they know how much hard work is involved in bringing up a child," said Susan, blushing at the thought that Dickon and Ben's arrival was inconvenient.

"Martha is much better here," decided Charlie, "with a loving extended family." He did not say that Martha might not take too kindly to going anywhere else.

"I could not imagine school without her," said Susan with a fond smile, "but will you try and find Martha's mother?"

"I don't see the point. I don't think it would help Martha. The letter seemed so hard – look after the baby because she is your responsibility, not because the mother is so desperate she has to give away the baby she loves to save them both, or to give the baby a chance of a better life."

"Will you tell everyone who Martha's father really is?"

"It would be cowardly to accuse a dead man who cannot answer back. It isn't his fault, girls always liked him and this one must have got him cornered. I think Benjie's secrets should die with him, except for people who need to know."

"What will you do?" asked Susan, although she thought she knew the answer.

"I will be responsible for Martha until she marries or is apprenticed," replied Charlie, "but she will be my daughter for the rest of her life."

Susan looked at Charlie, and realised that he was the man she had always loved. He thought he might have been Martha's father, but what young man didn't take what was offered? The important thing was that he gave Martha a good home and would not let her go into the workhouse, whether she was his daughter or not. She wanted to tell everyone how wonderful Charlie was, but she got stopped in her tracks.

"I hope people don't find out that Martha is not my daughter," warned Charlie, "or they will think I am a soft touch. Everyone and her grandmother would be leaving their baskets on my doorstep."

Susan was not taken in by the flippant remark, but resolved to keep her silence. She looked at Charlie, his thick black hair, bright blue eyes and nose that was slightly hooked, a face that was the image of Martha's. Susan would marry him tomorrow if he asked. He was going to ask, wasn't he?

29 THE RECONCILIATION

Charlie thought that everything was straightforward, and then started to wonder whether he needed advice. Tom would know the answer, but he wasn't due back for another week and Charlie was worrying away in the meantime, because he had lied inadvertently when he registered the baby with the information that he had at the time. The question was not whether or not he had been lying but how much it mattered, and there was only one person who could tell him.

As Charlie walked down the street towards the registry, Susan appeared out of nowhere and walked with him. She had one of those new caps, like some of the more fashionable younger girls, instead of the sturdy bonnet that she usually wore. Susan seemed to be everywhere that day; she had called in at the shop twice for things that could have been delivered, and he had even caught a glimpse of her when he went to the pie shop for his dinner.

The street was very busy; it seemed that people were hurrying to the shops before they closed, but he felt that everyone was looking at them as they walked together on the cobbles. Susan said that she was on her way to the draper's to get a ribbon for her new cap, and did he like her new headgear. Charlie said that it was very attractive, and reflected that the shops would all go out of business if it wasn't for women prettying themselves up with things that they didn't need.

Charlie waited at the back of the registry to make sure that he was the last customer and would not be overheard. He was rewarded when the registrar dismissed his clerks, invited Charlie into his own office and offered him a nip of brandy to keep the cold out.

"Is this just a social visit, or are you here for some other reason? I thought that Miss Graham was going to be a real old maid, but now they say she's bought a fancy cap," said the registrar, careful not to say anything about mutton dressed as lamb.

"Miss Graham is a handsome woman and she would be a good wife for anybody."

"Well, just whom has she set that fine cap at?" mused the registrar, peering at Charlie over his spectacles.

"I wouldn't know." Charlie was unsure of where the conversation was leading. "I came to ask your advice about Martha."

"Oh, yes, the whole town remembers the day that you registered her," said the registrar with a smile. "Is she still causing disruption? Or have you found out who her mother is?"

"We still don't know who Martha's mother is, but Jeannie found a note in her basket. I honestly thought that Martha was my daughter, but it seems I was mistaken. The basket was left on my doorstep because I was her late father's next of kin. And it looks as if Martha was born in Westmorland."

"You would be within you rights to send her to the workhouse," started the registrar.

"Perish the thought, who would look after me in my old age? I just wondered if I needed to adopt Martha to make things legal."

"I could change the records, but I wouldn't advise it, especially if she wasn't born locally. Just in case she needs help from the parish later on, when she is older, you never know. Presumably you are still her next of kin, unless her birth has already been registered somewhere else."

"Is it possible to find out? Are there records like yours all over the country? Could you find out whether a girl Martha's age was born in Hilltop without me having to go there and ask questions?"

"Hilltop, is it?" asked the registrar, looking sharply at Charlie. "Your cousin Benjie was a naughty boy."

"I would rather nobody else knows that I am bringing up another man's child. I don't want any more baskets left on my doorstep. Susan is only just speaking to me as it is."

"Leave it with me, I shall find out your answer myself and not involve my staff. I shall keep silent unless Martha wants to marry one of her half-brothers, then allege an impediment to the marriage. I haven't had a chance to do that yet. Come back next Friday and you will have the answer to your question."

Charlie was on his way home, when he met Arthur, who seemed to pop up out of nowhere and was very interested in where he'd just come from.

"What brings you to the registry?" asked Arthur, as he knew that there were no recent deaths to register. "Are you planning a wedding? Mind you, Susan is getting on a bit now; she looks as if she will be large like her sisters. My Sam wonders whether she'll have to go through doors sideways."

"Susan is a fine figure of a woman, very imposing; if Sam was still at school she'd have him caned for a remark like that. Sorry to disappoint you but I was just visiting an old friend and I have no plans for a wedding."

"I just thought you might book the ale house for the party, before we get too busy. I wasn't prying."

***

Charlie had a letter to say that Tom was due back, so Thursday was a frenzy of activity. Charlie and Ben decided to spruce up the shop; this would also encourage flagging trade and anyway the back rooms were a bit of a lost cause. Ben was cleaning and shining all the bottles, including the large jars of coloured ink that had pride of place in the window and hinted at magical cures. Charlie was busy making up extra cough syrup, tonic and little pills that would make a person feel better without being clear on what aspect of health was actually being improved.

Martha had called in, but was promptly sent to deliver tonic to Elizabeth Corrie, mystery pills to Sally and a bottle of something for 'Granny Coughdrop's' aching joints. Ben was too busy to do the deliveries and Martha liked to have an excuse to call in at the sweet shop. Charlie had decided to place the 'things that people might just fancy' near the counter so that customers couldn't miss them, and was starting with an enticing display of tobacco and pipes.

"I have come for my Sally's pills," said Kit who had just come in. "I was coming past so I thought I might save young Ben a trip. I can see he is busy; those bottles look really good from in here."

"Martha took the pills about half an hour ago," said Charlie, "but perhaps you would like to get your tobacco while you are here."

"My usual then please, and have you any baby's gripe water, we've run out again. The other children seem to like it; they make the baby laugh and queue up for gripe water when Sally brings it out for the baby's hiccups. Before I forget, Sally asked if you would all like to come to us for your Sunday dinner. Susan will be there. I must warn you though, Susan can be a bit difficult to live with and her temper is uncertain these days."

Charlie noticed Ben stop work, and his shoulders slump, so he sent him outside to clean the shop window.

"Susan knows her own mind, and she is used to a class of children that obey her every whim, so after school she forgets where she is and expects everyone else to obey without question," said Charlie, as he found a few bottles in a dark corner. This batch had sold out very quickly as Ben was bit heavy handed with the alcohol as he made it up. "You had better take two bottles as we haven't much left. We'll see you on Sunday. Dr. Tom should be back as well."

Charlie was putting gripe water and laudanum in a more prominent place to tempt the customers, when Adam Corrie came in, followed by Martha carrying an enormous paper bag.

"I have come for my wife's tonic; she is a bit out of sorts at the moment."

"Martha's already delivered it," said Charlie, looking at Martha who nodded as she fiddled with the scales at the back of the shop, "but if Mrs. Corrie is out of sorts perhaps she might try senna, it has just come in and is very effective." Charlie turned away so that Adam would not see him blowing the dust off the packet.

"Thank you, perhaps she'll give it a try," said Adam. "I heard a rumour that you and Miss Graham might be getting married; I wish you all the best but I've worked with her for a while. If you stand up to her, she won't walk all over you, but it would be hard work doing it all the time."

"Miss Graham is a strong capable woman who won't be cheated by tradesmen or be weeping and wailing over every little problem," boasted Charlie. "Any man would be proud to have her as a wife."

"Rather you than me," warned Adam as he left, "don't say I didn't put you in the picture."

There was a loud thump from the scales, and Charlie looked to see what Martha was doing. She had put the large paper bag on one side of the scales and had taken the two-ounce weight off the other one to replace it with the four-ounce weight. Martha finally weighed the sweets against the eight-ounce weight, but they were a little bit over.

"You have very good measure there," said Charlie.

"Granny Coughdrop is giving up the shop and going away so she was trying to clear things out," announced Martha. "I asked if I could help so she gave me all these."

"When is she going?" asked Charlie, remembering that Granny Coughdrop had a large bill to settle.

"As soon as she can clear everything out, and then nobody will sell sweets anymore," replied Martha, taking a sweet out of the bag and eating it while the scales wobbled. "There is a nice clear corner over there so Ben and I think we could sell lots of sweets in this shop. I could work in the shop like Sam works at the draper's, and weigh the sweets out for you." She took another sweet out of the bag; the scales balanced perfectly and she looked up with a smile.

"You have a lot to learn before you become a shop assistant. I wouldn't want you eating all the profits," said Charlie. "I will see Dr. Tom about it when he gets back."

"See me about what?" asked Tom as he came back unexpectedly early and wondered what was happening to the shop.

∗∗∗

The next day Charlie set off down the street with lightness in his step; he had been pleased and surprised to see Tom looking so well. He had thought that Tom was very poorly, as he had not returned home or answered letters – it had never occurred to him that both Tom and the letters were marooned in Hilltop by the snow. Charlie and Tom were on their way to see Granny Coughdrop about her unpaid bill, to see if they could come to some arrangement to pay in kind rather than by coin.

"Hilltop must have done you good," said Charlie. "Perhaps you just had a bad chill and not consumption at all."

"We'll never know," replied Tom. "Did you want to call at the registry since we are passing, and they seem quiet?"

The registrar was on his own in his office, a napkin tucked under his chin and a large plate of bread, cheese and pickles in front of him. He got up to shake hands, but the napkin stayed in place as a reminder of the more important activity that should be taking place.

"What can I do for you gentlemen?" asked the registrar. "A wedding perhaps? To a difficult lady who has worn out her welcome at both churches but could get married here?"

"The wedding is not being planned yet," said Charlie, who had persuaded Tom to accompany him on his errand to avoid being buttonholed by Susan, "but please remember that the lady in question has had a very difficult time over the past few years and I don't think I've helped any. I came to see if Martha has another birth certificate somewhere, as you said you could find out."

"There is no other certificate for her so I suggest you leave things as they are, there's no need to change the father's name since her real father is no longer with us," answered the registrar, looking at his plate. "Presumably Benjie is buried in Hilltop."

"Dr. Tom couldn't find any record of a burial there. I don't suppose you could find the death certificate for us; we think it was potato picking week in 1838," said Charlie, "that would give a clue to where he was buried, so that his sons could pay their respects."

"I will see what I can do, but perhaps the lads could pay their respects to both parents at their mother's grave at the meantime," replied the registrar, as he picked up his knife and fork.

"We are not sure where that is either," said Tom, "my brother-in-law works for a newspaper and is trying to find out for me but has had no success do far. It's all a bit of a mystery."

The registrar settled down to his dinner again. Charlie and Tom took the hint and set off for the sweetshop.

***

"Come on, Ben, they will be waiting for us at the forge and Sunday dinner will be getting cold," nagged Tom.

"Coming," answered Ben as he staggered downstairs with a large bundle of belongings.

"Where are you taking all those?" asked Charlie.

"I thought that the surgery might be a bit crowded when you're married," pleaded Ben, "and I could spend more time with Dickon."

"Take those things back at once," ordered Tom sternly, while trying to keep his face straight. "You're a surgeon's apprentice and your place is here with us."

"But wouldn't it be better to…" started Ben.

"No it wouldn't," said Tom. "Off you go!"

Ben took his belongings back to his room, they could hear him dropping things on the stairs and complaining under his breath that he didn't want to live in the same house as that battle-axe.

"Had you thought about where the happy couple would be living?" asked Tom when Ben was out of earshot. "Susan would be very welcome here but she might not like it."

"I hadn't thought that far ahead," said Charlie, "but you are right, she wouldn't like it. She would go through the place like a dose of salts, everything would be dusted and swept, and we wouldn't know the place. Even poor Yorick would be polished and none of us would get any rest."

Both men shuddered.

"That's one of the reasons I didn't marry Nancy, all those years ago," said Tom.

"You have the comfort of your family here, without having to raise a family of your own. It is different for a poor orphan with no kin, but I can see that marriage would take a lot of getting used to," said Charlie. "I think Susan and I should have our own house, and I could just be here during the day and when I'm on call."

"Or when you need a bit of peace."

Charlie's face brightened.

"Let's go and get it over with," he said.

30 THE ANSWER

"Well, if you're really sure," said the registrar, "I will make arrangements for the wedding. Banns or licence?"

"I suppose it had better be licence." Charlie looked at Tom, who had come with him for moral support. "Neither of us attend Church regularly now, and we don't have to announce the fact that we are getting married."

"Arthur will do that once Susan has made arrangements for the party," said Tom.

"I think Arthur has told everyone already; they knew before we did," said Charlie, as he watched the registrar write with his beautiful clear hand. Charlie always had great trouble reading his own writing, but Ben had learnt to decipher it as he made up the medicines. Tom's writing was even worse. He could see that there were some trades where a man's handwriting could matter.

"Cat got your tongue?" asked the registrar.

"I was admiring your writing," answered Charlie. "I wish I had paid more attention in class."

"People will need to read my writing for years to come," explained the registrar, "a man may want information about his forebears, now that people move away to work and lose touch with their families. The information helps the government find out about us, to try and improve matters, but I can't see that happening."

"The government are getting really nosy; there was that census in 1841 asking where people lived and what they did which is none of the government's business," said Tom, "and I can't imagine anybody not knowing who their ancestors were."

"In your family, perhaps, everything was done properly, but it's a wise child who knows his own father. In the past things were written in the parish register, and there were none of these boxes to write in. If the entry said something like 'Martha, reputed daughter of Charlie Armstrong', the poor law guardians knew who to chase for money," said the registrar. "Now people are much cagier and don't admit paternity until the child's marriage, and then they expect the child to help to support the father."

"But the new system must have some advantages," mused Charlie, "otherwise they wouldn't have put it in."

"New things very rarely make things better," grumbled Tom, "they just make everybody more work."

"If there were no national records I would not have been able to make those enquiries for you," said the registrar.

"Did you find anything out?" asked Charlie

"Unfortunately not," answered the registrar. "There has been no death certificate for Benjie between now and the present day."

"That means he must be still alive after all this time!" said Charlie with a sudden surge of hope.

"There was no sign of him at Hilltop," said Tom.

"I think it's more likely that they forgot to register his death," explained the registrar. "It happens sometimes. Out in the sticks, they go back to the old ways. But the strange thing is there was no record of Nancy's death, and prisons are usually very particular in their records."

"So perhaps she was reprieved and is in a prison somewhere," mused Tom.

"You said she was not in Carlisle or Whitehaven," replied Charlie, "and she hasn't written to us."

"Perhaps young Henry will find out for us," said Tom. "Nancy might still be alive."

"There was a letter from Henry this morning, sent on from Hilltop," said Charlie, "but I wouldn't get your hopes up."

***

Tom rushed back to read his letter while Charlie went to the ale house as he had arranged with Susan. He found her in the middle of a heated discussion with Arthur about the plates that were to be used. Susan wanted glass and china to discourage people from throwing them. Arthur was more pragmatic and wanted wood and pewter so that there would be less damage to people and property when the inevitable food fight took place.

"I think that Tom and Ben can easily deal with bruises from wood and pewter missiles," said Charlie. "I don't want to spend my wedding night patching up injuries."

"Whatever you think best," agreed Susan. "Now, about the fiddler. We want to keep the dancing going, and we can't do that if the fiddler can't keep sober."

"He's a good man," countered Arthur, "he only has one little weakness."

"He's unreliable," said Susan, firmly.

"You would sell more ale if the dancing kept going longer, Arthur," said Charlie, diplomatically.

"I sell a lot of ale when he's there," said Arthur, sulkily, "mainly to him. It would more than make up."

"How about hiring another fiddler so that they can share the work," suggested Charlie, as Susan was looking stubborn and it was looking as if the discussion would take all morning.

"I am glad that's settled, and now we can talk about important things like pies," started Susan. "The meat pies were all gristle last time, and there was nowhere near enough sugar with the gooseberries. If your staff can't make pies, why don't you get them from the shop like everybody else?"

Charlie sighed; it was going to be a long morning after all.

***

Charlie sat down wearily when he got home and he was grateful for the refreshing tankard of ale that Tom passed to him. He loved Susan very much, of course, but would be glad to spend time at the surgery when he was on call, or there was a remote possibility that he might be on call. The surgery kitchen was familiar and comforting, and he was glad that it would stay that way for a while.

"I had a strange letter from Henry," said Tom, passing the letter to Charlie, "It was not what I expected at all."

```
Dear Tom
There is a record of Nancy Armstrong being tried
for murder at Whitehaven, but no record of her
death at any jail in this county. I am trying to
find  out  whether  she  is  still  imprisoned
somewhere.
Yours
Henry
```

"It's very short," said Charlie, "and doesn't tell us anything we don't already know. But wouldn't she still be in touch if she was alive?"

"He doesn't say anything about the trial either," answered Tom. "I couldn't get much information at Hilltop, and it's not clear at all what happened on that terrible day. I didn't want to know details when I last spoke to Henry, because I feared the worst, and that Nancy had gone to the gallows regretting what she had done to Benjie. But now I would like to know who Nancy was supposed to have killed, and what happened to Benjie."

"Nancy could have been protecting Benjie," said Charlie, "not that it did either of them any good."

"She was a fine woman, and the boys should be proud of her," said Tom, "but we won't say anything to them just yet. I will write and ask Henry first. He might find Nancy in Westmorland or even Northumberland, but it is more likely that death records are missing."

"Susan has invited Mary Ann and Henry to the wedding," said Charlie, "so we can talk to him then, and see if he has found out anything else."

31 THE WHITEWASH

The wedding was due to take place the next day and Susan could not settle. She had given her house a really good clean so that she could impress people when she received her first calls as a married woman, but when she looked she could see things she had missed now the daylight was getting stronger. A particular cobweb in the corner was annoying her, so she got a stool to stand on, and picked up the cobweb brush.

Once she looked closely into the corner where the cobweb used to be, she could see a bit of whitewashing she had missed. It won't take long for whitewash to dry, she thought, but she ended up doing more than she expected as the new fresh whitewash did not blend in with the rest of the wall. When she had finished, the rest of the walls looked comparatively shabby and Susan thought that she had plenty of whitewash mixed and could easily do the rest of the room before the light failed.

Susan had not expected to see Jeannie that morning, but suddenly there she was, helping to move furniture.

"I thought you were going to hire a woman to help with the heavy work," said Jeannie as they moved the table.

"I haven't managed to find one yet, I don't know why," replied Susan, who was not sure that she wanted to hand over control of any of her cleaning to someone else.

"I am sure there must be someone out there who can do the heavy work for you," suggested Jeannie, although she had heard people say Susan might be difficult to work for.

"I hadn't expected to see you today." Susan took the plates off the dresser and put them on the table.

"I came to see you about the other cottage. Mrs. Jepson wants to move sooner rather than later, and I'm ready to move in."

"How soon?" asked Susan, as they started to walk the dresser away from the wall.

"Today! Old man Fosdyke says Rebecca can move in to his house straight away, separate rooms of course and with her grandmother as chaperone. The wedding is arranged for next week."

"But I won't have time to clean in between tenants, like I usually do." Susan wondered when she could fit in the extra work, and whether she had been a bit hasty starting the whitewashing.

"I'll do that," offered Jeannie. "It won't be much work, not like the last family with all those children."

Susan shuddered at the memory of the last cleaning she did at the second cottage, and she was exhausted after they finished moving the heavy dresser.

"I would be very grateful," said Susan, surprised to realize that she could not do everything herself, "your first week will be rent free. What made the Jepsons decide to move so soon?"

"I think they'd run out of coal, and old man Fosdyke was keen for them to move in as soon as possible."

"He must think it will be cheaper than paying them for all the knitting they're doing for the shop, "said Susan, moving the whitewash bucket, "but I'm pleased for Rebecca. She was one of the school's brightest pupils until she had measles and lost most of her sight. We thought the Jepsons would have to go into the workhouse until they managed to make a living knitting for the drapers. It's just a pity that he's so old, he looks about ninety."

"Arthur can remember him leaving Sunday School so he could be in his forties, but he says he was like an old man even then," said Jeannie, handing her the brush, "I suppose they are just marrying for companionship."

"And to save him money," said Susan, as she stood on the stool and started whitewashing. "The Jepsons' knitting is perfect, almost as good as those baby clothes of Martha's. Er... will Martha be moving with you? Charlie never mentioned her living with us, but she would be very welcome of course."

"Charlie should have said, she'll share a bed with Deborah in the second bedroom," said Jeannie, as she held the bucket while Susan finished the top. "Jack is away most of the time and his Uncle Tom says there is a bed for him at the surgery whenever he wants; he brings him tobacco back from Virginia when he can. Martha wanted to move into the surgery as well but Charlie put his foot down."

"You seem to have arranged it all between you," grumbled Susan, who would have preferred to be consulted.

"You don't want other people's children under your feet when you are first married," soothed Jeannie, "as you will soon have enough of your own."

Deborah and Martha arrived with bundles of belongings and asked where to put them, so Jeannie had to rush off to make sure that the Jepsons had moved out and the girls would not get in the way. Susan stepped down off the stool and worked on the rest of the wall, irritated that everything had been settled before she had been told what was happening. She did not want to start married life in the surgery, or share a house with Tom, Ben or Martha but she would like to have been asked.

The decision had been taken out of her hands, somehow, and she had no responsibility for it. There would be no reproach that she was too mean spirited to take on the surgery and all the waifs and strays like Ben, Martha and Jack. The day seemed to be getting away from Susan a bit, and she realized that from now on she would not have the control over her life that she had over her class. She just hoped that there would be someone to help her with the dresser when the wall was dry.

***

There were many people visiting briefly, looking for Charlie or Jeannie or the Jepsons, and it was early evening before Susan finished everything to her satisfaction. The room looked much better, and she hoped that the whitewash would not look too patchy in the daylight. But the next visitor was Mary Ann, very elegantly dressed and obviously not in the habit of moving furniture.

"Can you help me move this dresser back to the wall?" asked Susan, hopefully.

"I'll send Henry to do it later, there's no hurry. But look at the state of you, it's going to take ages for me to make you look beautiful for your wedding tomorrow," replied Mary Ann. "I've brought you a hat and everything."

"When will Henry help with the dresser?" asked Susan, ignoring the inference about her looks. She had given up on making herself look beautiful; she just concentrated on looking tidy.

"He had some news for Tom and Charlie," said Mary Ann, "and he should be here soon. You'll be the centre of attention tomorrow; you must look your best."

"What news does he have for Charlie?" asked Susan, as she picked up the kettle.

"I wasn't supposed to tell you yet but it's about Nancy's transportation," said Mary Ann, taking the kettle from Susan before she dropped it.

"Nancy's what?" exclaimed Susan as she sank down into a chair.

"She was never hanged; she was transported instead. They hadn't enough women prisoners and the ship was due to leave, so they took all the condemned women from the prisons, including Nancy," said Mary Ann, rescuing the hat from being squashed. "Henry is really clever and managed to find it all out for Tom, even though it was really difficult."

"So Nancy could still be alive somewhere," mused Susan, as she tried to take it in.

She had never quite admitted to the feeling that if she had been a bit more welcoming when Nancy visited, perhaps she would have not gone back so soon and the tragic set of events would not have started. But the thought that Nancy had been given a second chance, even if just for a short time, lifted a burden from her that she did not know she had.

"I wouldn't get your hopes up," said Mary Ann, kindly, "even if she survived the voyage she might not have lived through years as an indentured servant on the other side of the world."

"Would it be Virginia?" asked Susan, wondering how Nancy must have felt when she was told that instead of facing the gallows she had the chance of life overseas. Nancy had always liked adventure and excitement, and was not averse to starting a new life away from her friends and family; she had already done so once.

"They don't send prisoners there anymore, since the revolution," said Mary Ann. "I can't remember where Henry said it was and it is unlikely she is still alive. Now, what did you say you were wearing tomorrow?"

Susan was still in shock and allowed herself to be led away to the bedroom to look at her best outfit. All the time the outfit was being tried on, examined, tutted at, let out and tried on again, Susan was thinking about Nancy and how life was full of surprises and things you could not control: a lost cause could come good. In the distance, and it seemed miles away, she could hear furniture being moved, thumps, bangs, muffled curses and raised voices but no serious crashes or broken crockery. Susan was amused by a discussion between Martha, who wanted to open the shop the next day, and Charlie, who insisted that it should remain shut. For the first time for years Susan stepped back and let everything just happen on its own, and her spirits soared.

32 THE REGISTRY

Waiting in the registry, Charlie felt that he had been in this situation before. This was the sad little office where he had helped people register so many deaths; for some of the elderly death had been a blessing but so many babies had only been on this earth a very short time. Charlie used to look at the sorrowing family and he just didn't know why God wanted to snatch babies back so soon. He tried to chase gloomy thoughts away, by thinking of Martha's registration and the discomfiture of the clerk, and he felt a bit better.

He heard the crowd outside, and was surprised that so many people turned up to see him married, and could hear shouts of 'Good old Charlie Sawbones' and one or two saying 'Watch your back'. This took him back to his first attempt at getting married to Susan - he hoped that Sally and Mary Ann would make sure that she was not carrying a bouquet this time. He was glad that Susan was a strong woman who would stand her ground at the market, and be able to hear about his working day without fainting. If she scolded too much, he could always escape back to the surgery for a little while.

Charlie dragged his mind back to the present. The registry office looked as if it had been cleaned and polished specially and there was even a little jar of drooping flowers on the registrar's desk. Charlie tried to concentrate on what Tom and the registrar were talking about.

"So you can only find out about births, marriages and deaths in this country, not overseas?" asked Tom.

"I am sorry I can't help you," explained the registrar. "They all have their different way of doing things; there is usually some sort of record of an event but I wouldn't know who to contact. Whereabouts is it?"

"The penal colony near Botany Bay," said Henry, "all the way on the other side of the world."

"The only way is to find someone who is going, and in a position to…"

"Better you than me, Charlie, marrying that battle-axe," said someone from the crowd, and Charlie couldn't help himself but cringe, waiting for the missile. Instead there was a gasp from the crowd, followed by murmuring and he turned to look. Susan was walking towards him, escorted by Kit and followed by Sally and Mary Ann, and she looked beautiful. It was as if all the troubles of the past few years had never happened, Susan looked as she did before the arrival of Martha, before her sister disappeared and before her father died. Charlie expected her to wear her Sunday best but somehow it looked different, and her new hat was amazing; she was actually smiling and there was lightness in her step that he had not seen for a long time.

*****

True to his word, the fiddler had brought his son to help him out with the music towards the end of the festivities in case he felt a bit tired. The lad's playing deteriorated during the evening as he wandered too near the ale jug but he managed to keep going as best he could. Surprisingly Susan had found the whole thing very funny, especially when the old fiddler was discovered in the washhouse.

He was so completely out of it that they propped him up in a corner to watch as he drifted in and out of consciousness, and Charlie was very surprised that Susan was happy with this arrangement rather than using the horse trough to sober him up. The dancing faltered a little and some people were starting to lob a few pies at each other. Arthur's pies were ideal for throwing and bounced off the walls in a very satisfactory way. There would have been a major food fight if everyone had not been distracted by a new arrival.

Jack had changed since Charlie last saw him and he had a proper sailor's rolling gait, as if the floor was a deck that was going to move under him. He also had a pigtail; it was only three inches long but it had more than its fair share of tar. Deborah and the other children made much of him, and he taught them a song, and soon everyone was joining in the chorus of "Hooray, up she rises, early in the morning."

Susan was watching, smiling and tapping her feet, so Charlie turned his attention to the young fiddler who was listening to the words of the song with concern.

"That's what they do to drunken sailors, there are things much worse than the horse trough," warned Charlie, "now you come outside with me and let's see if we can clear your head. You will feel better after some fresh air."

The lad felt queasy when he went outside, but that resolved itself in the usual way and he felt ready to go back. The singing continued, the children were dancing but Martha was encumbered with a large slate that she carried with her. Jack had run out of verses and surprisingly the fiddler offered to play a hornpipe for him. Everyone was very impressed with Jack's dancing but Susan said that he just looked as if he was shaking water out of his shoes.

The wedding dancing started again. Jack was glad of a rest, and a place was found for him at top table so that Tom could ask him the all-important question.

"Did you remember my tobacco?" asked Tom, hopefully.

"Finest Virginia, much better than you sell in your shop," said Jack. "I hear you're selling sweets as well these days."

"That was Martha's idea," replied Ben. "Once Charlie persuaded her to give good measure and not put her thumb on the scales she was fine."

"What has she brought that slate for?" asked Susan.

"She sulked a bit when Charlie said the shop was closed and she didn't want to lose any sales," answered Ben, "so she is writing down the medicines that people want."

"She has sound commercial instincts," said Tom, "just like her namesake."

The children had stated a new game. Deborah was 'it'; she was questioning the other children but Charlie was too far away to hear the words.

"Are you going back to Virginia after your shore leave?" Tom asked Jack.

"I am bound for New South Wales, so I will be away a long time," answered Jack. "I don't think they grow tobacco and I probably won't be able to bring back anything useful."

Charlie wondered where New South Wales was; he knew it was not the same as old south Wales because Jack would have returned fairly quickly. The children's voices seemed to get louder. There was a loud argument over whether someone had said 'Pork and Beans' or not.

"Where exactly is New South Wales?" asked Tom. "It sounds very exciting if it's a long way away."

Ben went into a long monologue about the South Seas, Captain Cook, the Empire, botany, cannibals and Tom's eyes glazed over. Charlie felt that there was something at the back of his mind that he was trying to remember but the children were louder, possibly because Martha was 'it' and her voice carried.

"A sailor came from Botany Bay- what will you give him for dinner today?" asked Martha, approaching top table.

"Pickled cabbage and ships biscuits," grumbled Jack, resentfully.

"You are it! You didn't say 'Pork and Beans'," announced Martha triumphantly.

"I'm a sailor bound for Botany Bay and they hardly ever give us pork and beans," retorted Jack. "It would be very nice if they did. Only meat we get is the weevils in the biscuits."

Susan rounded up the children and told them in no uncertain terms to play their game somewhere else, but Martha wanted to ask about weevils. Charlie looked at Tom as the truth dawned on both of them and Tom's face lit up.

"There is something very useful that you could bring us from Botany Bay," suggested Charlie. "I will call in the morning and talk about it."

"That is all right, no need to disturb you in the morning, you will need your rest," replied Tom. "I can give Jack all the details."

33 THE SAILOR

Jack returned over a year later; the roll was more pronounced and the pigtail had grown to a respectable length. Charlie saw him in the distance, as he stood outside the church following the Fosdyke christening, discussing a bet with Arthur.

"Who would have thought it?" asked Charlie. "It looked like a marriage of convenience."

"Sam says that he's doing all the work in the shop now, and the old man has nothing else to do," said Arthur. "There's another baby on the way, apparently. We can settle up now if you like."

"It looks as if you have a secondary bet," replied Charlie, who had fished his book out of his pocket, and found Arthur's page. "Old man Fosdyke will ask everyone back for hospitality after the christening; you had very good odds on that one."

"Can you afford to pay out on both?" asked Arthur, "these must be difficult times for you. Not so many people in the town to need doctoring."

"We manage somehow," replied Charlie. Martha's sweets had been a success and the betting had always provided a steady income - he always covered himself when he calculated his odds.

Old man Fosdyke came out of the church proudly carrying the baby, but went home with just his wife and her grandmother and no hangers on.

"That makes us quits then," said Charlie. "Hello, Jack, good to see you after all this time, you're looking well."

"I've news for you and your family," announced Jack who was beaming all over his face.

"I could have sworn that Fosdyke would ask us all back for a cup of tea. Sam said that he had mellowed and had nearly given his staff a day off last Christmas," said Arthur. "News, did you say, young Jack?"

But Charlie was already shepherding his family and colleagues towards the forge; he knew that Deborah would tell Sam the news eventually but he wanted the family to hear it first.

"That's all right Sally, you sit and listen to Jack's news, Deborah and I will make the tea if you tell me where everything is," ordered Jeannie. "We can talk to Jack later."

Deborah would have preferred to hear the news but she did as she was told. Kit and Dickon were finding stools for everyone, it was a squeeze getting them all in but they could manage if the children sat on the doorstep at teatime. They were playing sailors outside; they each had their handkerchief tied on to a stick and they rolled as they walked.

"Did you find Nancy?" asked Susan, as she looked up at Jack; his eyes were shining and he was nodding. "Is she well?"

"She is very well! So is Benjie, and their little boy!" replied Jack amid gasps of astonishment from everyone. "Grand little lad about the same age as Martha, fair hair, very lanky, not like anyone in either family."

Sally, Kit and Dickon were hugging and jumping up and down, which caused a lot of disturbance and everyone had to hold on to their teacups.

"Benjie is alive!" said Susan.

"Yes, they were both transported. Benjie says that Nancy was accused unjustly, but he deserved what he got," said Jack. "Maybe this letter will shed some light."

He opened the bundle on his stick, and handed her a letter written in Nancy's clear hand.

Dear Sally and Susan,

When I went home after I last saw you, we had a terrible misfortune. Benjie was very late back from the manor, so I went to find him; it was terrible, the squire was horsewhipping him! I cannot tell you why - you are too young. Benjie was on the ground, bleeding and barely conscious and the squire kept going. I thought he was going to kill him so I picked up the pitchfork, just to threaten the squire and make him stop. The squire just took one look and then he fell down dead. I swear I didn't touch him but he deserved to die anyway.

The rest you know. I was tried and sentenced, a rich man can cause the ruin of a poor family very easily, and the squire's sons must have bought witnesses. I thought Benjie was dead and I cannot tell you how he managed to survive his beating, but he did and then he was sent out with the next lot of men prisoners.

Be careful, keep out of trouble, and look after your men. It is so easy to upset gentlefolk, and then they can take a terrible revenge with no one to stop them.

With love from

Nancy

"She was so brave," said Susan thoughtfully after Sally had read out the letter, "risking everything to save Benjie, and she nearly paid with her life. How she must have felt when she thought it was all for nothing and that he was going to die anyway."

"And when she was told that her life had been spared? And when she found out where she was going? And that Benjie had survived!" exclaimed Sally.

"Will they come back, do you think?" asked Charlie, when everyone had taken in the news and marvelled at what Nancy had done.

"Prisoners don't usually come back; by the time they have served seven or fourteen years as indentured servants, they've settled. It's usually difficult to find money for the passage home," said Jack, "so I drew a picture of them for you."

He handed them a charcoal picture that had a likeness of the three missing family members; it was not an expert drawing but they could see who the people were meant to be. Nancy looked a little older, but there was a liveliness about her that she had not had on her last visit. Charlie was relieved to find that Benjie looked just the same as he always had.

"Wherever did you learn to draw like that?" asked Jeannie.

"Mr. Corrie taught me in my last year at school when Ben was reading all those awful dusty books," Jack answered his mother.

"Their little boy looks just like you did when you were little," said Jeannie, dabbing her eyes with the corner of her pinafore.

"They called him 'John'," said Jack.

Tom's face was unreadable.

"Funny name, I can't remember a John in our family," mused Sally, "is it an Armstrong name?"

"I can't remember," replied Charlie, "any more letters in that bundle of yours?"

"This letter's for Dickon and Tommy," said Jack. "It's a long time since you were called 'Tommy', do you remember all the trouble when…"

"It is the name his parents gave him," said Susan.

"You had better read this letter, it is not addressed to me," said Ben, handing the letter to Dickon. This time the letter was printed and Dickon could read it aloud without a struggle.

Dear Dickon and Tommy

Your father and I are alive and well on the other side of the world. We do not think we will be able to go back to England as we are indentured for fourteen years.

Now we are making a life for ourselves in this strange and wonderful land, where there are mice as big as bears, spiders as big as birds and snakes as big as coils of rope. There are strange trees with flowers - they don't lose their leaves in the winter – and they even have their seasons the wrong way around. The weather is so hot and dry; there are times when I really miss the refreshing wind and rain.

Be good, learn well, and do not let girls get you into trouble.

Love from
Mam, Dad and your brother John (who has heard all about you)

"Mam was very brave and she saved dad's life but she writes as if we were little children," said Ben.

"I thought the same about our letter," said Susan, and they shared a conspiratorial glance. Unlike Dickon and Sally, she had been half expecting this news. Dickon was still puzzling over something.

"How can girls get you into trouble?" he asked.

Deborah giggled, and her mother gave her a sharp look.

"You'd be surprised," said Charlie, winking at Ben, and deliberately not looking at Tom.

"There are three more letters; one for Charlie, two for Tom," said Jack, handing over letters that went straight into the recipients' pockets, "and I can take letters back on my next trip."

"Aren't you going to read your letters now?" asked Deborah.

"We have to go back to the surgery," explained Tom. "The carpenter's daughter is expecting her first."

"And old Mrs. Jepson is looking very frail," added Charlie, "we could both be called out tonight."

"And I'll need to man the shop if they're both out," added Ben, who remembered that there was a book about Captain Cook's travels on the shelf behind Yorick.

"Surely you have time to finish your tea," invited Sally, producing a large cake out of nowhere, and cutting substantial slices.

"We can all finish our tea," decided Susan, "all three surgeons are busy but I can stay a bit longer." She beamed at Sally, waiting for an opportunity to give her a hug.

***

Tom opened his letter from Nancy by the firelight in the surgery kitchen, while Charlie was lighting candles.

Dear Tom

I give you heartfelt thanks for your help during a very difficult time; you gave comfort when I was alone and accused. I was a little sharp with you at the time because I did not want to break down and be unable to meet my end with dignity.

I was expecting to be led to the gallows the next morning, but instead I was taken to a ship full of women prisoners which was ready to set sail. I will not talk about the privations of the voyage, it took so long to get there, but I was so grateful to be alive and enjoying a second chance. We were sent to Botany Bay so some of the men prisoners could marry and become easier to handle but when it was my turn to be stared at, there was Benjie saying that we were already married! They didn't believe him so we went through a second ceremony, just in case. I was so sure that Benjie would never survive his injuries. I am still amazed that he is here with me!

Life has been good to us in this foreign land and at Easter we were blessed with a son. I am sure he is yours so he is called John after your father. Benjie has brought him up as his, because I don't think he knows.

Yours with thanks and affection, Nancy

Tom looked for Ben; he was out on the scullery doorstep reading a book in the last of the daylight. Tom handed Charlie the letter without a word, and started reading his second letter.

Dear Tom
I am sure John is your son but I have brought him up as mine. If he had been my son, Nancy would have known at her trial and pleaded her belly to be spared the rope. John must be a week or two younger and, looking at him, he could only be yours.
I am happy to bring John up as mine. He is a blessing when we have lost so much.
Yours truly,
Benjie

"John after his grandfather," announced Tom, "my father would be proud to have all those boys named after him, there are three 'John Harrisons' with Robert's John, George's Jack and Joe's Johnny. Then Mary Ann's John McKay and this one."

"Does Benjie know?" asked Charlie, wondering whether it was deception or Benjie's good nature that made him care for John.

"Yes, he does," replied Tom, "and he is content."

Charlie waited until Ben was in bed before he turned to the final letter.

Dear Charlie
I was working for My Lady. She had dainty ways and when she invited me into her bed it would have been churlish to refuse. The Squire found out and gave me the horsewhipping I deserved. I

played dead so he would stop, like I learnt all those years ago, but he kept on. Nancy waved a pitchfork at the Squire and he dropped dead, just like that! She got me home on the cart, I got down and I can't remember any more until I woke up in My Lady's bed. She woke me to say Mr. Percy and Mr. Peregrine were coming and I had to run. She did not dare to hide me anymore or she would be thrown out. I got as far as the barn before I collapsed, was shackled and taken by night to a prison ship.
It is a rare man that will bring up another man's child as his own. I am very grateful to you for looking after my daughter and I am sorry if it was inconvenient. I thought you would have called her Maria after your mother but from what Jack says, Martha is the right name for her.
I hope she has brought as much joy to you as John has brought to us.
Your cousin Benjie

"So now we know who Martha's mother was," said Charlie, passing the letter to Tom.

"According to Joe, Milady is living in seclusion in the Dower House; she has no friends and no family," replied Tom.

"She must be terrified in case the news reaches the gossips, then the squire's sons would turn her out and she'd go to the workhouse," said Charlie.

"Will you ever tell Martha who her mother is?" asked Tom.

"Probably not, "said Charlie, "as it's best if she doesn't meet her mother. Martha would be very disappointed in the way that her mother behaved. Milady nearly caused Benjie's death, not once but twice. Then she abandoned Martha to a stranger, and that could have been fatal. Susan and Jeannie have been much better mothers to that child than Milady could ever be. Benjie is a different matter, but he's on the other side of the world and I can always send him news of Martha. It looks as if money and being a lady does not give a girl many advantages, just more opportunity to make mistakes. Martha has a good family here; she doesn't need any one else."

BIBLIOGRAPHY

The main sources are the 1841 and 1851 England Censuses, for information about work and population movements in the first half of the nineteenth century. The information was supplemented by general reference books: *Our Ancestors Lived* by David Hey, *Albion's People - English Society 1714-1815* by David Rule and *A Social History of England* by Asa Briggs. The internet gave me a vast quantity of information about historical events, court records, working conditions, games and pastimes. I read *A History of Wigton* by T.W. Carrick for the development of a typical small Cumbrian mill town, but the fictitious town is smaller and situated further south. I read Dombey and Son, Mary Barton, Middlemarch and several other early Victorian novels to give me further background information.

ABOUT THE AUTHOR

Selina Stanger never got the hang of joined up writing so she became an author late in life.

She worked in IT for a small private company, took a career break, worked free-lance on computer games and magazines, and then got a hair-cut for a proper job in the civil service.

Selina is now retired, living on the south coast and enjoying the sunshine.

Printed in Great Britain
by Amazon